"Are you married?"

His gaze locked with hers. "No."

She swallowed, then asked, "Girlfriend?"

"No. I'm as single as a person can be," he said, with a hint of pain that tugged at her heart. His pale eyes returned to hers. He swallowed. "What about you, Renata?"

"Same as you," she said, her voice wavering. "Good thing, too, since I can tell you want to kiss me."

There it was again, that surprise that widened his gaze. Right before the corner of his mouth quirked up. "I do?" His voice was lovely, all gruff and gravel.

"Yes." She'd learned how to fake confidence from her four brothers—something she was incredibly grateful for.

He turned to face her, leaning against the railing as his gaze swept her from head to toe. "Do you want to be kissed?"

Dear Reader,

Renata Boone finally has her book! Since book one of the Boone series, her big heart and vitality assured me she must have her own love story. And now it's here. Renata is a strong, responsible and independent woman. So her instant attraction to a near stranger and the night they share together is not only out of character, it changes everything.

Ash's heart was so broken by the loss of his wife, being open to love—putting himself out there—wasn't an option. But he never anticipated meeting a woman like Renata Boone. Everything about her was unexpected in the best way. Their night together stirred up all sorts of things he wasn't ready to face, so leaving made sense.

When fate puts these two together again, the whole town is set on seeing them married and settled down. But Renata won't settle for anything short of love. And love is the one thing Ash isn't sure he can give her.

I've so enjoyed sharing this wonderful family with you. I hope Renata's happy ending closes out the series with a big red bow and happy smiles.

Wishing you the very best,

Sasha Summers

HOME *on the* RANCH

TEXAS WEDDING

— ✠ —

SASHA SUMMERS

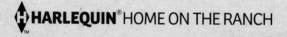
HARLEQUIN® HOME ON THE RANCH

Recycling programs
for this product may
not exist in your area.

ISBN-13: 978-1-335-47488-9

Home on the Ranch: Texas Wedding

Copyright © 2019 by Sasha Best

Printed in U.S.A.

Sasha Summers grew up surrounded by books. Her passions have always been storytelling, romance and travel—passions she's used to write more than twenty romance novels and novellas. Now a bestselling and award-winning author, Sasha continues to fall a little in love with each hero she writes, from easy-on-the-eyes cowboys and sexy alpha-male werewolves to heroes of truly mythic proportions. She believes that everyone should have their happily-ever-after—in fiction and real life.

Sasha lives in the suburbs of Texas Hill Country with her amazing family and her beloved grumpy cat, Gerard, The Feline Overlord. She looks forward to hearing from fans and hopes you'll visit her online: on Facebook at Sasha Summers Author, on Twitter, @sashawrites, or email her at sashasummersauthor@gmail.com.

Books by Sasha Summers

Harlequin Western Romance

The Boones of Texas

A Cowboy's Christmas Reunion
Twins for the Rebel Cowboy
Courted by the Cowboy
A Cowboy to Call Daddy
A Son for the Cowboy
Cowboy Lullaby
Her Cowboy's Triplets

Visit the Author Profile page
at Harlequin.com for more titles.

To my amazing editor, Johanna.

Thank you for your insight, your patience
and your friendship.

Chapter 1

"Move over, Santa Claus," Renata said, patting her blue-gray mare, Luna, on the neck. A final click on her phone screen and she'd officially checked everyone off her Christmas list—early. With all the babies and weddings they'd seen the past few years there was a good chance she'd emptied her bank account in the process. Come Christmas morning, it would be worth it. "I even got something for you, Luna. A cowgirl is only as good as her horse."

Luna snorted, navigating the shallow creek with ease and keeping a slow and even pace. Renata glanced over her shoulder to make sure the two horses she was bringing back to the barn were still following them. They were. They probably felt the chill in the air, too. Nothing like the unexpected threat of an ice storm to make even the most rebellious horse eager to get back to the ranch. It was October. In Texas. The temperatures normally hovered in the mideighties for another month.

She shivered and tugged up the thick flannel-lined collar of her coat. After her two-hour search, she'd earned a cup of hot chocolate in front of the fire—preferably in her flannel pj's. This weekend was her last bit of downtime. Thanksgiving might be weeks away, but Monday Stonewall Crossing would officially begin its annual holiday craziness. The only thing on her calendar was tomorrow's Ag Club meeting. It was her nephew Eli's freshman year. If he wanted her to be there, she would. Besides, she loved helping out with the holiday floats—it was one of her favorite things about this time of year.

She loved the holidays—loved how busy she was. Nothing like being busy to keep gut-wrenching loneliness away. Since she wasn't one to wallow in self-pity, she made sure to stay occupied. Besides the Christmas parades and the town Gingerbread Festival, she had a stack of invites to holiday parties and get-togethers to fill her waking hours.

One thing she could check off her list: Christmas shopping.

"And since I have the best presents, I will continue to be everyone's favorite aunt," she said to Luna.

Luna snorted, her ears flicking.

"I'm glad you agree. I can live with being the cool aunt." That was enough. It should be enough. But every time she saw one of her brothers with his wife, saw the adoring looks and stolen touches, she ached. She wanted that, desperately. An unwavering love connecting her to that one special person, tying them together for the world to know and see. And a baby of her own.

Nope. Not going there. She'd focus on being thrilled that her four brothers were so happily settled. They deserved happiness. From now on, she was going to ignore every twinge of envy being surrounded by her nieces and nephews and blissfully content brothers and their wives stirred. Being single wasn't the end of the world. She had plenty of friends and family that loved her. Better to concentrate on being the best sister, the best daughter and the very best aunt in the great state of Texas. Yes, that was a good plan. No point wishing her life away.

Her humming grew louder and she sat up straight in the saddle. She and Luna led the horses up the hill and across the pasture to the fence line. Her brother Archer had asked her to check this stretch of wire. It was the oldest, showing signs of rust and wear, but he was hoping the replacement could wait until spring. "Archer will be happy," she murmured, seeing no cause for concern.

They'd moved down the fence when Renata spied a white truck parked on the side of the road. It had pulled well off into the grass, close to the fence line. The cab was elevated and the front passenger wheel was missing. Rental plates.

"Where's the driver?" she asked, nudging Luna into a faster clip.

A few hundred feet down the fence, she had her answer.

A large canvas duffel bag and seen-better-days black felt cowboy hat lay in the brittle winter grass at his booted feet. He was tall, his red flannel shirt encasing broad shoulders and a lean torso. Other than thick black hair, she couldn't see much. A camera covered most of his face. He was clicking away at the glorious fall sunset.

Luna's ears pivoted toward the man, the rapid-fire shutter echoing in the relative quiet of the country. Renata ran a hand along her horse's shoulder and glanced at the sunset. There was no denying the view was incredible. Vibrant blues, purples and pinks that colored the sky, shot through with bold strokes of yellow and orange. To her, Texas fall sunsets were just as impressive as Vermont's turning leaves. But then she loved her state, the Hill Country and her hometown. Stonewall Crossing was beautiful no matter what time of the year it was. And she appreciated anyone who recognized that.

"Evening," she said, drawing Luna to a stop.

"Good evening," he said, setting his camera aside and grabbing her full attention.

Oh my. Pale eyes with thick lashes. A strong jaw covered in a dark stubble. He was all strong angles, in the very best way. Strong. Manly. And super good-looking. The sort of good-looking it was easy to stare at. Like now. She was totally staring at him. "Need help?"

He grinned, the corners of his pale eyes crinkling just right. "I think I'm lost."

He was lost. And she was staring. She blinked, hoping he hadn't picked up on her dazed-with-admiration episode. "It's wide-open country with twisty farm roads," she agreed. "Folks get lost all the time. Take one wrong turn and you get stuck on Loop 8 or wind up back on the highway."

"Sounds about right." Was she imaging things or was he staring right back?

She tipped her hat back, trying her best to stop staring. He was handsome, so what? She cleared her throat, nodding at the pasture behind her. "And there's not much out here. Most cows are leery of talking to strangers and offering up directions," she teased.

His eyes widened before he laughed. "I've noticed. They've all been giving me the cold shoulder." His gaze held hers. "I'm Ash."

"Renata."

He was studying her face. Intent. Curious. Interested.

She blew out the breath lodged tight in her chest. "Where are you headed?"

He cleared his throat, then blinked, effectively severing their connection. "Stonewall Crossing. Staying at a place called the Lodge."

"The Lodge?" Her home sweet home? Looked like things just got more interesting. "You're almost there. About another mile and a half down the road on your right. There's a big gate—you can't miss it."

He pulled his gaze from hers, searching the long stretch of road. "So, I was close?"

"Yes, sir. Not so lost after all."

His gaze traveled across the sky before returning to her. "I don't mind getting lost now and then. That's when you find sunsets like this."

"And meet new people, too, I'd imagine."

He nodded. "If I'm lucky." His smile took the chill out of the air and sparked the surface of her nerves. "Since the cows are no help."

Say goodbye. Ride off. Sitting here, making small talk, with the temp dropping, was ridiculous. But she didn't want to ride off. "You're a photographer?"

He shrugged.

She shot a pointed look at the camera.

"Hobby." He chuckled.

"We get a lot of naturalists out here. Lots of birds and wildlife." She forced her eyes from his, to sweep the land she so loved. She could almost see it in spring, awash with color. "You should come back in the spring. These fields are covered in bluebonnets, red Castilleja and black-eyed Susan." She glanced back in time to see the muscle in his jaw clenched tight, the heat in his eyes startling her.

"I'll have to keep that in mind." His voice was gruff. And her stomach tightened.

What was happening?

Luna nudged her boot with her nose, snorting. Her horse's patience was running out. She nodded. "I'm assuming that's your rental truck back there?" Meaning he wouldn't be in town long.

He sighed. "No spare."

"Might be worth making a complaint. Especially since you're stranded and we're expecting snow." She gazed up at the sky. It didn't look like snow. "Once I get the horses taken care of, I can come back for you," she said, patting Luna again. "Luna's getting impatient. Dinnertime and all."

He seemed to think about it, his gaze exploring her features before he finally said, "I don't mind the walk. But I appreciate the offer."

"You sure?" she asked, ignoring the tug of disappointment. Not like she wouldn't see him again.

His jaw muscle tightened again. "I'm sure," he added, shouldering his bag and putting his cowboy hat on. It might be on the worn side but he wore it well.

She'd have time to decide whether or not she liked it later. After the horses were home and safe. She touched the brim of her hat with her finger and smiled. "Hope you get some good shots before the sun goes down. Not many lights out here—then it gets *dark* dark out. Take care."

"Thanks." His pale gaze searched hers. "Nice meeting you, Renata."

With a nod, she nudged Luna forward and the horse set off at a fast trot. The hammering of her heart had nothing to do with their ride back. Fifteen minutes ago, she'd been resigned to accepting her fate as the cool single aunt in her family. Now she wanted to spend a little more time having Ash look at her like that—with his clenched jaw and brooding pale gaze. She thought a night with him might just provide the sort of memories that could comfort a woman for a lifetime. He looked the type.

And now she'd officially crossed the line into ridiculousness. It had been a long time since she'd been on a date and, obviously, the loneliness was getting to her. He was gorgeous and interested and she was sort of vibrating from the charged connection between them. But…she wasn't that sort of girl.

Even if, for the first time ever, she really wished she could be.

John-Asher was in no hurry. After his run-in with Renata, he needed to clear his head. He'd been too heartsick to notice the opposite sex, until now. And now, well, he hadn't really had a choice. She'd sort of demanded his attention. Magnetic. Hypnotic. Whatever. It felt like she'd reached inside, grabbed hold of something long dormant and shaken it wide-awake. In ten minutes flat.

He shivered, the nip in the air biting right through his flannel button-down and the undershirt beneath. It was fatigue. Period. The mind could play tricks on the body. And that's exactly what had happened. A pretty girl. A friendly smile. A few laughs… She was being neighborly, nothing more. But she'd made his crappy day better.

Since it was unlikely their paths would ever cross again—which was good—there was no cause for concern.

This visit was pointless. After his interview at the Virginia-Maryland College of Veterinary Medicine, he knew what his first pick was. He was a damn fine diagnostician and a well-regarded veterinarian, and they appreciated that. But the University of East Texas

Veterinary Teaching Hospital, right here in Stonewall Crossing, had been Shanna's top pick. She'd researched every candidate town's schools, its history and crime rates, and the potential for him to have a long-term career. *This* was the place she'd wanted to raise Curtis, the place she'd thought they could call home. And, even though she'd been gone for almost two years, the urge to make her happy hadn't faded. He'd made her a promise. And he kept his promises.

He shifted his duffel bag from one shoulder to the next and pushed his favorite felt cowboy hat down. The ache in his chest was constant and familiar. At times it would fade and he'd fight to hold on to it. If the ache was gone, Shanna would be gone. And that wasn't something he was willing to accept yet. A jagged knot lodged itself in his throat, making his eyes burn.

She wanted him to be happy—dammit, he was trying—but it was too soon for him to contemplate moving on. He and Shanna had had something special. She'd been his wife and best friend, the one who'd plucked a small-town country boy from the saddle and introduced him to the wonders of the world. Her zest for life had been contagious. Without her…life was hard. In the beginning, getting out of bed had been a challenge.

Curtis was a balm to his soul. His son was the light of his life. With his all-consuming smiles and his joyful giggles, that little boy was all Ash needed to keep moving. Hurting or not, he'd be the best father he could be for his boy.

Their family might be small, but it was strong. The

two of them would do just fine on their own—no matter what his mother and mother-in-law might think.

His half-hearted attempts to move on failed epically. Online dating was a bust. Blind dates a no go. He'd even hit a club or two with his single friends but quickly realized he wasn't interested in a hookup. Besides, he'd yet to meet a woman who sparked his interest. A memory of Renata smiling popped up so quickly he bit out a curse.

Until today. And that spark had been so bright it had scared him. If he was being honest, it was more than a spark. *More like a bonfire.* He ran a hand along the back of his neck, rolling his head to ease the tension, and glared up at the wide-open sky and the first flicker of stars.

Her quirky humor. Her smile. Those blue eyes. Altogether too tempting for a man in his position. And he'd let her ride off. No, he'd hoped she'd ride off. Because he wasn't ready. How could he be? It wasn't right.

Frustration twisted his insides.

The Lodge rose up, its windows spilling welcome light into the growing darkness. It was bigger than he'd pictured, more impressive, and likely warmer than the cold night air. The bite in the air had increased along this last stretch of road. His fingers tingled and his nose was downright numb. He *almost* wished he'd taken Renata up on her offer of a ride.

Almost.

Spending more time with her might have ended the fascination—or added to it. She might be the most beautiful woman he'd ever seen, besides Shanna. And, looking at her, he'd felt something he'd thought he'd lost with his wife. Attraction. Real, hard, knock-the-air-out-his-lungs attraction.

Why was he surprised? He was lonely. So damn lonely he ached. But feeling this way after ten minutes with a stranger was unsettling. And out of character. He wasn't a hormonal teenager, dammit. He had responsibilities and a family to take care of.

He hurried up the Lodge steps and pushed through the thick wooden door, appreciating the instant warmth, smell of baking bread and bright light. A hot meal, a hot shower and a soft, warm bed was all he wanted. Tomorrow he'd have his interview and leave. And he wouldn't spend another minute thinking about Renata.

"Evening," the middle-aged woman gushed. "Checking in?"

Five minutes later he'd dumped his duffel bag on the massive king-size bed in his guest room. The place embraced the country-rustic style. He hung his hat on the wooden headboard, eyed the bed and thick quilt with appreciation, and grabbed the plate of fresh-baked chocolate chip cookies on the bedside table. Yes, please. He popped one into his mouth and moaned. Homemade and warm. He ate another and headed into the bathroom for a shower. Pearl, the lady at the front desk, had told him dinner was being served—just enough time to clean up *and* warm up.

The waterfall shower was heaven. He stood under the steaming faucet until he could feel his fingers and nose again then toweled off and dressed for dinner, leaving the last two cookies for a bedtime snack.

Pearl greeted him at the dining room door. "We have chicken-fried steak with cream gravy, mashed potatoes, and fresh green beans or chicken pot pie." She paused. "Or we've got a soup and salad bar? But you look more like a meat-and-potatoes man to me."

He wasn't sure what a meat-and-potatoes man looked like, but she was right. "Chicken-fried steak." He was in Texas. Might as well enjoy the local food.

"You're in for a treat." She pointed to the back wall. "There are cups there, tea, soda, water or coffee. Help yourself and pick a spot."

He nodded, poured himself a cup of steaming hot coffee and sat in a booth along the back wall. A quick inspection of the room told him it was filling up so, to avoid conversation, he opened the information packet the University of East Texas had sent to him. He was excited about teaching—about working with the best and the brightest while keeping a family-friendly schedule.

His phone vibrated, a picture of Curtis appearing. He ran his finger over the picture. Weight settled on his chest as he studied the sweet face. Curtis, sitting between Ash's mother and mother-in-law, grinning his adorable grin at the camera. His mother followed up with an All good here. Good luck at your interview tomorrow. We'll see you soon text.

Curtis was getting big—running and climbing and getting into everything. Lucky for him, his son had a sweet disposition and an adventurous spirit. And no fear. Just like his mother. He didn't like being away from him but knew the short trip, the flights and unfamiliar surroundings would only throw off his schedule.

Thank you for keeping an eye on him, he texted back. Since Shanna's death, his mom and Shanna's mom, Betty, had all but moved in. They were both widowed, both retired and both smitten with their only grandchild. As invasive as they were, he knew he couldn't do it without them. When he'd gone back to work, they'd waved off his suggestions of day care to watch Curtis instead. Which suited Ash, and Curtis, just fine. Shanna had planned on staying home, and the mothers were so tickled by the arrangement, the only thing he had to worry about was Curtis getting spoiled. So far, there was no cause for concern.

"Your dinner." The blue-haired waitress put a massive plate piled high with deliciousness in front of him. "Dig in, honey. Nothing like a full stomach to make a man smile. I guarantee you that there will put a big smile on your face." She pointed at the food. "Let me know if you need anything else."

He nodded and took a bite. Flavor assaulted his taste buds. The waitress was right. He was smiling. And *good* didn't begin to describe it. When she returned to drop off a heaping basket of still-warm dinner rolls to his table and winked, he nodded his approval. She chuckled and headed on to another table. Another table with a certain blonde cowgirl. Sitting alone, staring at a computer screen.

He froze midchew. Renata.

Damn it all.

Instant awareness tightened his body. *No.* She was just a woman. No different than any woman he passed on the street. Certainly nothing to get worked up over.

Nothing special. His training had taught him to analyze problems, face them head-on and find answers. Maybe looking at Renata that way would help him. He blew out a slow breath, set his fork down and really looked at her.

There was no denying she was beautiful—she was. And the way she smiled up at the waitress had him wishing she was smiling at him.

Dammit.

Even if he were in a place to pursue her, someone like her would have someone. He waited, expecting her better half to join her. But, as he did his best to eat every morsel of his meal while subtly watching, she remained alone. Even staring at her computer screen, her face was animated.

Enough. He finished his dinner, gulped down the last of his coffee and hurried from the dining room without a backward glance. It was too early to sleep, but maybe he'd have an easier time focusing on the university's information packet from the comfort of his room and that big bed—far from distractions. Especially blue-eyed blondes with dazzling smiles.

After an hour of reading all about the impressive equipment, accolades and experienced staff at the University of East Texas Veterinary Teaching Hospital, and another hour of lying there flipping channels on the television, he grew restless and his brain began to wander. Never a good thing. Curtis was safe. The mothers had everything under control. The rest needed to stay locked up tight. Best way to do that was to occupy himself. Did they have a gym? He'd packed on some muscle recently, spending more time than he'd admit working through his anger and grief.

He pushed out of his bed and peered out the window of his room. The view from his bedroom window was clear, the sky lit up with a thousand diamonds of various size. Perfect material for a photo session. Carrying his coat in one hand and his camera in the other, he headed down the hall into the great room.

It was quiet, save the occasional snap and pop of the fire in the massive fireplace. An older gentleman sat dozing, a paper held in his hands. Other than that, he had the place to himself. Ash slipped by, taking care to open the French doors that led out onto the back porch. The view took his breath away. It was so familiar and so alien all at once. Yes, he and Shanna had traveled through Stonewall Crossing, but it was more than that. The rolling hills reminded him of his childhood home.

He'd grown up on a southern Oklahoma farm. He'd spent his days on horseback, digging post holes, learning every inch of the place until he could walk it blindfolded. As a child, he'd had free rein of the wide-open, with the added comfort of a sometimes-too-close-knit community. After his father's death his mom had held on to the place as long as she could. In the end, she'd had no choice but to sell. She'd bought the small house she still lived in and used the rest to put him through college. As thankful as he was, he regretted losing his heritage. Especially on nights like this. To have a peaceful view like this every night would be a blessing.

Finger on the button, he peered through the lens, angling for the best shot.

"Glad to see you didn't freeze on your walk." Renata.

He should be surprised. So why wasn't he?

He hadn't left his room to find her. He'd left his room because he was restless. She had nothing to do with that. But there was a part of him that knew he was lying to himself. And finding her here stirred up all sorts of emotions. Should he make small talk? Or bolt back inside?

She waited, rocking silently, her long blond hair pulled over one shoulder and a cup of something steaming in her hands. At ease and relaxed. Unlike him. Standing here, alone with her, he was wound tight and barely holding on. Not that he could say any of that to her. The longer she waited, the more her smile faded. What the hell was wrong with him?

If he kept staring at her, he'd scare her. He didn't want to scare her. "I managed to keep all my fingers and toes," he managed, his voice gruff and thick.

"Glad to hear it. I imagine taking pictures would be hard without them—your fingers I mean. Guess you don't need toes for it, though." Her smile returned. "And a night like tonight deserves to be photographed."

He studied her closely, unable to hold back the answering smile her teasing caused. Yes. Beautiful.

She stood, cradling her mug closer. "Want some hot chocolate?"

No. Not really. So why was he nodding?

"I'll get you some," she said, heading toward the door.

"I mean, no, I'm fine." Why the hell had he stopped her? If she went inside, he could leave—put distance between them. But if she left… "You're familiar with this place?" he asked.

Her smile changed, like she knew a secret. "A bit. Why?"

"Small talk, I guess." He wasn't good at this—talking for the sake of talking. Recently, he spent the majority of his time with two old women who never let him get a word in edgewise and a baby who was content to make random noises.

"What's your favorite thing to photograph?" she asked, leaning against the railing at his side.

He looked down at her as the wind kicked up. Her sweet scent flooded his nostrils and his brain. The ache was sharp and sudden. He'd almost forgotten this. The urge to touch a woman, to take her hand…or hold her close. But now, staring down at Renata, he wondered what it would be like to feel her in his arms. To run his fingers through her soft hair. Or breathe in her scent. To taste her lips and, for a little while, forget about heartache and loneliness.

Chapter 2

This big, gorgeous, brooding man wanted to kiss her. He'd been staring at her mouth so long she began to think he might just do it. Worse yet, she wasn't opposed to the idea. She wanted this big, gorgeous, brooding man to kiss her. Even the fact that he was a complete and total stranger wasn't a deterrent.

She'd never been one to act on attraction or take risks. And her uneventful and disappointing love life was the result. But tonight, with Ash, the connection between them was too tangible, electric and undeniable. The way he was looking at her—he might as well be touching her.

"Ash?" she whispered.

He blinked, swallowed and stepped back. "Jet lag," he muttered, running a hand over his face. But when he looked her way, his jaw tightened and his lips thinned.

He was embarrassed. He shouldn't be.

She'd never played games. Ever. When she was a kid, she'd asked for what she wanted—figuring the worst that could happen was being denied. This was the same thing, wasn't it? If he wanted to kiss her and she wanted to kiss him, they should. As long as there was no one and nothing stopping them? She cleared her throat, fully aware that he was trying not to look at her. "Are you married?"

His gaze locked with hers. "No."

She swallowed, then asked, "Girlfriend?"

"No. I'm as single as a person can be," he said, a hint of pain tugging at her heart. His pale eyes returned to hers. He swallowed. "What about you, Renata?"

"Same as you," she said, her voice wavering. "Good thing, too, since I can tell you want to kiss me."

There it was again, that surprise that widened his gaze. Right before the corner of his mouth quirked up. "I do?" His voice was lovely, all gruff and gravel.

"Yes." She'd learned how to fake confidence from her four brothers—something she was incredibly grateful for.

He turned to face her, leaning against the railing as his gaze swept her from toe to head. "Do you want to be kissed?"

Breathing was a challenge. How could a look make her feel so beautiful? He was waiting for an answer. "By you?" she asked, smiling.

He laughed then, a wonderful, full-chested laugh. "Were you out here waiting for someone else to come along?"

"I wasn't really waiting for anyone. I was enjoying the view. And my hot chocolate." She hesitated, then confessed, "But I was hoping you'd show up."

"Why?" There was a vulnerability that plucked at her heart.

She pointed up at the bunch of mistletoe she'd helped hang. It was several feet away from them but—she thought—close enough. There were several bunches placed in strategic spots around the porch. "Isn't it bad luck? Not to be kissed under the mistletoe, I mean."

His was laughing again. "I've never heard that." But he stepped closer.

"I'm sure I have," she said, setting her mug on the railing. "Might as well get it over with."

His brows rose. "You don't sound very optimistic."

"I'd rather you wanted to kiss me instead of doing it out of obligation." Was she being bold? Yes. But, if he kissed her, would it be worth it? Yes. Somehow, she knew it would be completely and totally worth it.

"So there's no confusion…" He stepped aside, put his camera on her rocking chair and pulled her another five feet away from under the mistletoe. "I want to kiss you."

His words made everything melt a little, in the best possible way. "Good answer," she said, breathless. And eager. Her heart went into overdrive in the beat department, but at least he couldn't hear it. His hand slid up her neck to cradle her cheek, leaving a trail of tingles and fire and warning and excitement and pure want in its wake.

Her hand covered his as he stooped to kiss her.

Oh. His lips… Her eyes fluttered shut as his thumb brushed along her jaw. She'd never kissed a stranger. To be completely honest, she hadn't kissed a lot of men. She was selective with her kisses.

But she was so glad. His mouth was firm, moving against hers with a tenderness that had her swaying into him. Gripping his shirtfront. Shuddering as his arms slid around her waist. Shuddering again when he pulled her flush against him. Her hand slid up, tangling in his thick, dark hair.

It was the best kiss ever. The sort of kiss that went on and on. She didn't want it to end. There was hunger in his touch—need. From the tremble of his hand at her waist, the hitch in his breath and the urgency of his mouth on hers. And when her lips parted beneath his, he held on to her like a man drowning.

Oh God, she understood. She didn't know his past but she knew the desperation. He was alone. She was alone. And this, being wrapped up in him, clinging to him, assured them, right now, they weren't alone. Both of them craved something more. Needed each other— in this moment if nothing else.

He tore his lips from hers. "I'm sorry," he whispered, gasping. "It's been a long time."

"Don't apologize." She stared up at him, knowing her eyes blazed with just as much hunger as his. Her fingers traced along his hairline, down his temple and along his jaw. A jaw that tightened briefly. "Wow. That was some kiss."

"It was," he ground out, his voice hard. Whatever he was thinking, he stiffened. His arms stayed anchored around her waist. But he leaned away from her, as if he was fighting some internal battle. His pale eyes closed, his hands and fingers pressing against her back, before he relaxed. When his eyes opened, the fire burned bright. "You've been straight with me—"

"Because I wanted you to kiss me," she interrupted, her hands resting on his shoulders now. She didn't want to let go. She didn't want to say good-night. Not yet.

He smiled. "I'll be straight with you." He paused. "I'm here for one night." He cleared his throat. "But it seems to me we could both use the company. I want you something fierce." His gaze pinned hers. "Stay with me."

Stay with him. She could hold on to him all night. His hand slid up her back to sweep the hair from her shoulder. There was tenderness in his gaze and his touch. His kiss told her there would also be passion. Dammit, she ached to find passion with this man. She ached for him. A head-to-toe quiver racked her body at the mere thought of what they'd be like together.

She was pretty sure this wasn't how one-night stands were supposed to go. She'd seen enough movies and TV shows to know this was unusual. But she figured there was a reason for his hesitancy. There was pain in those pale eyes. He'd been badly hurt. Maybe he was still hurting. He might want to spend the night with her, but he didn't want there to be any misunderstanding or pain when they went back to their respective realities.

Tomorrow, he'd be gone and no one would ever know about her magical night.

She'd have a secret to treasure.

She didn't have to think about her answer. Every sensible bone in her body was inexplicably silent. There was no need for a pros-and-cons list or ticking through consequences. She wanted what he was offering, 100 percent. She wanted him—more than she'd ever wanted anything. "Yes."

He took her hand and led her toward the door.

"Your camera," she reminded him.

"Right." There was an adorable splash of red on his cheeks.

Minutes later, camera in hand, they were sneaking across the great room and down the hall to his room. She kept waiting for panic to set in—or to start second-guessing her decision. But his hand held hers, their fingers threaded, fitting together. This didn't happen to her. Men didn't blindside her this way. Or send an electric current through her body. But Ash did.

Whatever hesitation he might have felt evaporated once the door closed behind her. When his hands cupped her cheeks, she slid her arms around his neck. Lips locked, bodies straining, they made their way across the room to the bed. She kicked her boots off, almost tripping, but he caught her.

Her hands tugged the red flannel shirt from his pants to slide beneath the thick fabric. His skin was warm and smooth under her fingertips.

He had her shirt unbuttoned in no time. Once it was open, he sat on the bed and tugged her between his legs. "Damn," he moaned. His arms slid around her waist as he nuzzled the skin between her breasts. Wet kisses, the slide of his tongue along the edge of the cup…she wanted more. She reached behind her to free the clasp and shrugged out of her shirt and bra.

His breath powered out of him, one hand reaching up to cradle her full breast. His thumb caressed the peak before his mouth took over. His tongue brushed against the nipple, again and again, causing the throb between her legs to build. Her fingers twined in his hair. She pulled him closer as she arched into him. On and on, he lavished attention on every inch of each breast—driving her out of her mind with want.

His nose trailed along her side while his hand continued to tease and play with her breasts. The stroke of his tongue tracing her belly button was sweet torment. A soft moan tore free from her throat, causing him to look up at her and smile.

That smile. Her fingers tugged his hair and she bit her lip. Yes, she was enjoying this. Oh, so much. But then, so was he.

He unbuttoned her jeans and tugged them down her hips. She stood before him in nothing but her pink "It's Sunday" underwear.

"It's Friday," he said, glancing up at her. "Those have to go." With a grin, he tugged them down.

She was laughing when her panties went flying across the room.

"Better," he said, his gaze devouring her. But he wasn't touching her. The longer he stared, the more nervous she became. "You're beautiful, Renata." His words were magic. She felt beautiful standing there. When his gaze finally met hers, the want coursing through her veins grew unbearable. She lifted his hands and placed them at her waist, needing his touch as she tilted his head back and bent to kiss him.

He wasn't sure how they'd ended up here, but he was feeling like the luckiest son of a bitch on the planet. Tonight was theirs and he was going to savor every minute he had with her. She set him on fire. The feel of her hands sliding over his body. The soft moans and broken sighs. The stroke of her tongue against his. The slide of her silky hair falling over his shoulders. She made him remember he was a man. A living, breathing man with very human wants and needs.

He stood, the sensation of her naked breasts against his chest kicking up his heart rate. He might want to make this last, but his body wasn't going to make it much longer. It had been too long.

His flannel shirt joined hers somewhere on the floor. Boots, jeans, boxers, too. He didn't give her time to inspect him, though. He bore her back on the bed, groaning at the feel of skin on skin. He kissed her, his lips sealing tight and his tongue delving into the heat of her mouth. He lost himself in her. Her scent, her touch, the brush of her thigh against his hip... He settled between her legs but kept right on kissing her.

She met him, kiss for kiss. She arched and clung, her hands kneading his back and hips.

He couldn't wait, couldn't stop himself. He ended their kiss to watch her. When he slid deep, her reaction almost pushed him over the edge. Her moan, the way her head fell back and the sheer tightness of her body. He thrust once then stilled, breathing hard and fighting for control.

Her eyes fluttered open. Bright blue, even in the light of his bedside table. Her gold hair fanned across the white sheets. Her breasts shook with the power of her breathing. Her body cradled him deep, throbbing for him. Everything about her was vital. Beautiful. Healthy. He didn't want to think about Shanna now. Didn't want to remember how cancer had taken the pink from her cheeks and laid waste to her body.

"Ash," Renata whispered, her hand pressing against his cheek. "Kiss me."

His gaze held hers as their lips met, needing her to block out the rest. She smiled against his lips. When he arched into her, sliding deep, her moan dragged him firmly back to the present.

Tonight was about this. Living now. He was damn well going to take advantage of it.

Her fingers ground into his hips as he thrust into her again and again. And every time he fought to make sure it wasn't the last. When she fell apart beneath him, he watched, mesmerized. She turned into the pillow to muffle her cries but he nudged the pillow aside. He wanted to hear her, to know that he'd given her pleasure. It was all he needed to find his release. Pleasure poured over him, drowning him in her. She did this to him. She gave this to him. She made him *feel* for the first time in so long.

He collapsed beside her on the bed, the sound of ragged breathing filling his room.

When he looked at her, her eyes were closed. But

there was a smile on her face. He was smiling, too. Eventually, she looked at him, covered her face with her hands and giggled.

He laughed. What else could he do? She kept surprising him.

"This is…was…" She spoke through her hands.

"You said 'wow' earlier." He watched her, curious.

Her hands slid down to reveal those blue eyes. "That was when you kissed me."

He rolled onto his side, propping himself over her on his elbow. "Can't wait to hear how you describe this then."

Her eyes crinkled from the smile hidden behind her hands. "I have no words."

He smiled.

"This is the wildest night of my life." The crinkles lessened. "I've never done anything like this. Ever. Just in case you thought this was a normal Friday night for me."

He took her hand in his. "Me neither."

"I mean, I don't even know your last name or anything about you. Except you're a photographer." She swallowed. "And you're an incredible kisser. And… even better at this." Her smile was back.

He chuckled. "Well." It was nice to hear.

"Did I embarrass you?"

"No. Flattered." He squeezed her hand. "I think it's safe to say you turned my carefully planned trip into something entirely unexpected."

"And that's a good thing?"

He nodded, swallowing back the tightness in his

throat. He'd almost accepted he'd never feel anything that wasn't tinged with sadness. But now… Maybe there was hope. Eventually. "A very good thing." He stared down at her, memorizing her smile. She had the sort of smile that was contagious. A person would be broken not to smile back. He'd thought he was broken, but here he was, grinning like a fool.

"You're very tall."

"Where did that come from?" he asked.

"I'm tall. A lot of men would say too tall." Her eyes sparkled. "It was nice to reach up to kiss you is all."

Which seemed like a natural place to kiss her. A soft kiss, light, teasing—and the brush of his nose against hers. "You keep on throwing me curve balls."

"I've been told I'm a little too…forthright." She shrugged. "You grow up in a household as crowded and noisy as mine was, you learn to cut to the chase."

"I appreciate it. People talk too much, for the most part."

"Well, I've been accused of that, too." Her smile grew. "Not that there's been much talking tonight."

He grinned.

"Can you ride a horse?" She pointed at his favorite hat hanging on the headboard. "You have the hat and the boots, but there are plenty of people that come through Stonewall Crossing to play country for a while."

He laughed.

"What?"

She had no idea how charming she was. Even more

so considering she was naked and in his bed. "Nothing," he said, leaning down to kiss her again.

He liked the way her hands slid up his chest. Liked the way her fingers gripped his shoulders when his tongue slid between her lips. He liked pretty much everything about her. And loving her body… She had the sort of body a man could spend hours exploring. Thankfully, they still had what promised to be a long and sleepless night ahead of them.

"I'm glad your truck had a flat tire," she said between kisses.

He broke away from her, running his fingers through her long blond hair. "And I'm damn lucky you decided to sit on the porch, not waiting for me, to have your hot chocolate."

"You are," she said, pressing a kiss against his neck. "Damn lucky, I mean."

Her lips fastened to his neck and any hopes of a verbal response were gone. Every nerve was on fire for her again. She was right, he was damn lucky.

Chapter 3

Ash dismounted from the gray sorrel he'd ridden across the sprawling acres of Boone Ranch and led the horse into the barn.

"How long has it been since you've ridden?" Fisher asked, glancing back over his shoulder.

"Too long." The few hours on horseback had reminded him of just how much he loved it. "We sold our family place when I was in high school. After that, with school and all, I didn't have much opportunity."

"Must have been hard." Fisher's brow furrowed, the quick shake of his head sympathetic. "But now that'll change. The college uses horses sometimes, when they go out on calls. You find a horse here you like, we can work something out."

One more surprise. This place, these people—the

surprises kept coming. After a thorough tour of the school and his new office, Fisher had invited him back to his place for dinner with his family. Fisher's father had asked him to check a windmill and Ash had been all too happy to ride out with him. This was beautiful country. Wide-open and quiet. Things might not have worked out the way he'd planned but there was a reason.

There was no denying this was beautiful country, even now that winter had set in. And the town? Genuinely kind folk, full of charm and welcoming. After his last visit, he'd left this place knowing he'd never come back. After his night with Renata and the minefield of confusion he'd had to shut down the morning after, he'd had no choice.

Yet here I am.

"You good?" Fisher asked, beating his hat against his jean-clad thigh.

He nodded, pushing his hat back on his head and smoothing his shirt. "I should clean up before dinner."

Fisher grinned. "I have boys. A little more dirt won't hurt a thing." As soon as they reached the house, Fisher was greeted by shrieks and a flurry of activity. Ash watched, smiling at the open affection between father and sons. By the time the noise died down, a small boy was hanging off one of Fisher's arms, another sat on his boot—like the man was their personal plaything.

And Ash missed his son more than ever. "That's some greeting."

Fisher chuckled. "Thanks for your help today."

"Anytime." He cast a final glance behind them, the winter landscape barren yet gorgeous.

"Just remember you said that. There's always something needing extra hands. I'll warn you now, if my dad hears you say that, he'll find a way to put you up on the ranch full-time." He paused. "I'm dead serious," Fisher said, leading him farther inside. "Let me introduce my two monsters. Zac, say hello." He spoke to the boy on his boot.

"Hello," the boy said, his black hair standing on end.

"And this one—" Fisher lifted his arm so the other boy was dangling in the air and laughing "—is Nate. Nate, say hello."

"Hello," the boy said. "Who are you?"

"This is Dr. Carmichael," Fisher said. "He just moved here to work at the vet hospital with me and Uncle Hunter."

"Fixing animals?" Zac asked. .

Ash nodded. "Yep."

"Good," Nate said loudly.

"Boys." Fisher's pregnant wife shook her head. "Daddy's not a jungle gym. Come on, your bath is ready."

"Ash, this is my wife, Kylee." Fisher dropped an arm around her shoulders. "Kylee, Ash."

"I've heard a lot about you, Ash. To have the Boone brothers agree on something is no small thing so knowing they all wanted to hire you says quite a lot. Welcome to Stonewall Crossing. It's a great place to call home."

"Thank you." He shook her hand. "And thank you for the dinner invite."

"Glad you could make it. I'll apologize for the chaos now." She shook her head as the boys made a lap around the leather sofa. "Bath time, boys. Say good-night."

"You got this?" Fisher asked her.

"Of course." She rolled her eyes. "And then they go to bed." Her smile said it all.

Fisher chuckled and pressed a kiss to her temple before she corralled the boys down the hall.

"Cute kids," Ash said.

"They keep us running. Literally." Fisher yawned. "How about a beer?"

"Sure," Ash agreed, following him into the living room. "This is some place."

"One of the original structures on the property. Always something needing fixing, but it's home." He offered him a longneck. "Guess you're house hunting? Anything in mind?"

"It'd be nice to have some property." He chuckled. "Nothing to compare to this, of course." He'd learned today how significant the Boones were to the region. Not only were they the founding family of Stonewall Crossing *and* the veterinary hospital, they had one of the largest ranches in the Southwest. They were important folk. And, from what he could tell, truly decent people.

"I'll keep my ears open." Fisher pulled a plate of steaks from the refrigerator. "With so many folk looking to escape the big city, property gets snapped up pretty quick."

Which was understandable. There was a sense of traditional values, safety and community to the place that would be a haven for those tired of the tug-and-pull of larger cities. "I'd appreciate it."

"Grill's out back," Fisher said, opening the French doors and walking out onto the massive deck that ran the length of the house. Ash followed, pulling the doors closed behind them. "You were leaning toward working up north last time we talked. What changed your mind?"

His mother-in-law. Betty hadn't meant to turn down the job offer he'd received from the other university. She'd simply been trying to get on to Facebook—or so she said. But she'd opened half a dozen windows, downloaded "How to Speak Mandarin" software and, apparently, sent three words to the University dean. "No, thank you." By the time he'd called them back, the job was taken. When they realized what had happened, Betty had burst into tears and apologized for three hours straight.

Stonewall Crossing hadn't been his first choice but, after he'd cooled down enough to understand what had happened, he realized it was the best option. The town, the country, was great. The university, its facilities and staff were, too. Coming back…he'd been scared. It had been near impossible to leave the last time. He'd stood in that airport, staring at the flight-status boards, wondering what the hell he was doing. Because Renata had gotten to him.

Nope. Now was not the time to be thinking about her.

But, funny or not, admitting he'd wound up here due

to his mother-in-law's lack of computer skills might come off as offensive. Instead, he'd opted for a safe explanation. "In the end, it came down to where I saw myself long-term. Where I wanted to put down roots." He sipped his beer. "And the state-of-the-art equipment at the hospital didn't hurt, either."

Fisher chuckled. "Just wait till you get to use them." As he put the steaks on the grill, they talked about their work, what Ash could expect, the regular clients, the donors, the deans and this year's group of fourth-year students.

"I'm out," Fisher said, lifting his beer.

He nodded.

"I'll be back with a refill." He took the bottle and headed inside.

Ash leaned against the deck railing. On the hill, a buck stood silhouetted against the sky, casting a long shadow over the winter landscape. Damn, he wished he'd brought his camera. This would have made an incredible picture. He wasn't just being polite when he'd complimented Fisher on the view. No matter what angle, Ash would have something to shoot. And the setting sun, the slow retreat of light from the hills and fields, was breathtaking.

The back door opened. "Fisher's running a parent intervention, but I brought your refill."

He turned, fully expecting Fisher's wife.

But it wasn't Kylee.

It was the last person he'd expected to see here.

Renata?

His brain short-circuited a little. Sudden pressure,

like a kick from a steel-toed boot, slammed into his chest. How was she here? Standing there. Startled.

Just as he remembered—damn beautiful.

The beer bottle slipped from her fingers and went crashing to the wooden deck at her feet. It shattered, sending beer all over her boots and jeans. Not that she reacted. She didn't move. She just stood there, staring at him, the color draining from her cheeks.

"You okay?" Fisher yelled from somewhere inside.

Renata nodded. "Fine." But it was a whisper. "Well…" She swallowed. "You. You're here?"

He smiled. It was good to see her. "Hi."

Her brows rose. "Hi?" she asked, stepping back and crunching on glass. "Ash. What are you doing here?"

What the hell was he doing? At the moment, he was staring. Stunned. Trying like hell not to panic.

Fisher came through the back door. "What happened?" Fisher asked. "You okay?" he asked Renata. "You get cut? You look weird."

Ash was amazed at how quickly she pulled herself together. The way those blue eyes turned on Fisher as she teased, "Gosh, thanks. You know how to make a girl feel special."

"You're fine," Fisher said, surveying the damage at her feet. "Beer down, huh? I'll get the broom." He shook his head. "Now you've met another member of the Boone family. There's a lot of us but this one is special. Ash, this is my twin sister, Renata Boone."

Renata Boone. Twin sister? That answered a few questions he had…

Well, shit.

He'd slept with Fisher's twin? Men tended not to take kindly to their sister's flings. Not that he was a fling, exactly. It hadn't been a fling for him, anyway. Not that he knew what she was—or rather, what she had been—to him. And he didn't like it. He swallowed, doing his damnedest not to stare at her.

"Big sister," Renata shot back, taking pains to avoid eye contact with Ash.

"Whatever makes you feel better," Fisher said as he disappeared inside to get the broom.

Then those blue eyes fastened on him. "What are you doing here?"

"It's good to see you, too." He smiled.

Her eyes widened and her cheeks turned a lovely shade of red.

His hand ached to take hers. Instead, he flexed it, resting it on the railing and holding himself in place across the deck. Too far to touch her. He cleared his throat. "I'm the new teaching physician at the vet hospital."

"You are?" She blew out a deep breath. "You... *You're* Dr. Carmichael?"

He nodded, wishing he could get a read on her reaction.

"But..." She shook her head, her gaze searching his. "You said you were here for one night."

She was upset he was staying. He was upset she was Fisher's twin. And there was nothing they could do to make this less awkward. He'd hoped like hell he wouldn't run into her again, hadn't wanted to. Their time together had shaken him up—scared him. She made him feel…feel. If they ran into each other again, and he'd assumed that would be a *big* if, he'd figured he'd deal with it.

Wrong.

He wasn't equipped to deal with this. Her. Here. Now. The woman he dreamed about was staring at him with all the horror and confusion he was feeling. "My plans changed."

"So…you're staying? In Stonewall Crossing?" Her blue gaze searched his. "That won't change?"

No, it wouldn't. Of all the offers he'd received, this was the best. And Curtis? This place was kid friendly— a place Shanna had wanted for their son. He'd made peace with that. Now he was going to let his reaction to Renata Boone challenge that?

No. He was a grown man, for crying out loud. He'd get over whatever it was that she stirred inside him. Even if, looking at her now, that bone-deep want gripped him. *Dammit.* He'd have to be careful until he was over this. It wouldn't do to remember the brush of her lips on his neck or the hitch in her breath when he'd touched her the right way. His lungs ached for air and his fingernails gouged the deck railing. *Dammit. Stop. It. Now.* But he couldn't. Couldn't forget. Couldn't think. Or breathe. Or break the hold of the blue eyes he'd dreamed about.

"We'll get these steaks flipped." Fisher emerged, making them both jump. He offered the broom to Renata before turning his attention to the grill. "Almost done. You're not on some fancy diet or something, are you, Ash? Vegan, gluten-free, something or other?"

Fisher was expecting an answer. And openly staring at Renata probably wasn't the best idea, either. "No. I'm a meat-and-potatoes kind of guy." He did his best to laugh.

Renata didn't move. Those big blue eyes were fixed firmly on him. He was moving before he realized it, taking the broom from her. The burn of her fingers against his was a sweet reminder of the very thing he needed not to be thinking about right now. He frowned, sweeping the splintered glass into a pile.

"Earth to Renata?" Fisher turned. "You sure you're okay?"

"I'm fine," she said.

No, she wasn't. But only Ash knew why.

"Uh-huh. You're never this quiet." Fisher looked at Ash and shrugged. "Renata's a bigwig in town. The head of the Tourism Department—making people welcome is part of her job. She's a talker. Normally. Off to a rocky start, sis. First you drop his beer, then you don't say two words to him. Not very welcoming."

Her mouth fell open. "I didn't realize I was here on the clock, little brother. I thought I was here to have dinner with my family." She glanced at him then. "I am sorry for dropping your beer, Dr. Carmichael. And, of course, welcome to Stonewall Crossing. It's a great little town to call home."

"Ash, please." The knot in his throat didn't budge. The sooner his son arrived, the sooner Ash would feel more grounded—and less distracted. "I'm happy to be here," he said, toasting them with the refill Fisher had provided. "And thanks for dinner."

Fisher nodded. "Where are you staying?"

"The Lodge." Where he'd spent the most incredible night. With Fisher's sister. Dammit.

"My dad's place. And my sister's, too. She lives there—guess that makes you two roommates. Didn't you stay out there before? When you came for your interview?" Fisher was too busy piling the steaks onto a platter to see her reaction.

But Ash saw. She was breathing heavy and staring at the ground, her full lips parted slightly. When her gaze darted his way, the impact slammed into him. Heat coiled low in his belly, liquid fire, making the urge to reach for her threaten his calm. Especially now that she was within reach. He cleared his throat, took a sip of his beer and finally answered. "I did."

"I'm surprised you two didn't run into each other when you stayed there originally." Fisher carried the steaks inside, leaving the two of them alone on the deck.

Ash couldn't tear his gaze free. The longer they stared, the more weighted the air between them grew. Pressing in. If he didn't put space between them, he feared the same current that had landed them in bed the first time would lead them there again. It was real, fiery and undeniable. Knowing he was staying at the Lodge didn't help. *She* was at the Lodge.

It was a good thing he was a man of his word. One night, that was what they'd agreed on and that was the way it had to stay. For both of them.

The Lodge was a big place. If they were both careful, they'd avoid one another. No point in making things uncomfortable because they'd…slept together. It had happened. It was over. Their night together had been a beautiful fluke.

Still, the tiniest sliver of doubt remained.

What if it wasn't? What if the two of them, together, could be something…more? He tore his gaze from hers, forcing himself to follow Fisher into the house. He wasn't up for something more. He wasn't sure his heart would ever be up for it—even with someone as wonderful as Renata.

Renata couldn't stop talking.

John-Asher Carmichael sat across the table, looking for all the world like he was enjoying himself, while she was on the verge of falling apart. How did you behave when your one-night stand showed up for dinner at your brother's house and would now, apparently, be an everyday part of your life? Worse, how was she going to see him without thinking of and aching for the incredible things they'd done and shared? The hopes and dreams she'd poured out while she rested her head against his chest…

It was warm. Very warm. She plucked at the front of her shirt and glanced at the cuckoo clock on the wall. It was early yet—meaning she was stuck for a long, torturous dinner. Her only option? Apparently, put her Director of Tourism face on and gush like a fool. She tapped into every bit of interesting and not-so-interesting piece of information she could think of to help pass the time. Her nervous energy kept the words flowing—while preventing anyone else from really participating in the "conversation."

The longer she talked, the more confused Fisher looked.

Kylee appeared to be fighting laughter.

And Ash? Well, she was doing her best to look at the ornately framed bouquet of pressed, dried flowers over his left shoulder versus the actual man. If her gaze accidentally bounced off his, she sputtered to a stop and lost her train of thought.

"Pie?" Kylee asked, holding a piece directly in Renata's line of sight. "Maybe take a breath," she whispered.

Renata's stomach growled. She'd poked at her steak, mashed all the toppings into her plump baked potato and cut her green beans into bite-size pieces, but she was fairly certain she hadn't eaten a thing.

"Buttermilk pie is my sister's favorite," Fisher explained.

Ash said, "It does look delicious."

"I used your mother's recipe, too," Kylee said, setting the plate in front of her. "Eat," she mouthed.

Renata sighed. Fine. She'd eat.

She'd killed a good hour and a half with her aimless chatter. Dinner was done, and dessert signaled impending freedom. Besides, her face hurt from smiling and she was sick of the sound of her own voice.

"You're an encyclopedia on all things Stonewall Crossing, the Hill Country, and every plant, animal and water source in the region," Ash said, taking a bite of his pie.

"That was…something," Fisher agreed. "Felt like a test review or cram session. Planning on quizzing us later?"

He and Ash chuckled, pricking her pride. "Maybe I will." She scrambled for a logical explanation. "You know I…I take my job seriously." And she did. But that didn't explain her bizarre behavior this evening. Had she really listed off the reasons bluebonnets had become more prolific the last four years? And why oak wilt was such a threat to the Hill Country? She shoved a massive bite of pie into her mouth to prevent any further outbursts of random conversation.

"Renata can't help it. It's in their blood, I think. The Boones are tied to the land." Kylee smiled. "They love this place, the people—pretty much everything about it. The more time you spend with them, the more you'll learn."

"Can't say that I blame them. It's beautiful country." Ash glanced out the window. "Photography is my hobby—I can tell I'll have plenty of inspiration."

"Tell us about yourself, Ash. Where are you from?" Kylee asked.

Renata chewed slowly, giving herself permission to fully enjoy the bite of heaven in her mouth. She'd been fighting a stomach bug for a few days and hadn't eaten a thing all day. And now? She was upset, but this pie… Delicious. A slight groan escaped, drawing all eyes.

"Sorry." She covered her mouth with her hand.

But she didn't miss the tightening of Ash's jaw, or the whiteness of his knuckles as he held his fork. "I agree with Renata. This is the best pie I've ever eaten."

She nearly choked on her pie when he said her name. The husky timbre sent all sorts of warm tingles along every nerve ending. Her name, that tone, pulled an especially bone-melting memory front and center. Ash, braced over her, flushed and breathing heavy…saying her name. The temperature in the room shot up a good twenty degrees.

Fisher, on the other hand, was like a dog with a bone. "You're acting funny. You sure you're okay?"

She nodded, shoveling another bite of pie into her mouth.

"Maybe you're working too hard?" Fisher pushed. "Right now is one of the busiest times of year for her. Between parades and festivals, float and gingerbread competitions, she needs a holiday to recover from the holidays." Fisher shook his head, leaning toward Ash to continue. "She takes on too much sometimes."

She swallowed and smiled at her brother. "And you worry too much." Another bite of pie. No more talking. Talking was bad.

"Maybe. Maybe not. Blame it on the twin thing but you're keeping secrets, I can tell." Fisher was watching her. "And you don't keep secrets. Ever. So, yeah, I'm worrying. You tell me—should I?"

She froze, fork midair, stunned by her brother's intuition. She'd underestimated him. Seriously underestimated. She sucked in a deep breath, inhaling part of Kylee's delicious pie instead of swallowing it.

"Fisher." Kylee placed a hand on Fisher's arm, her dark eyes full of reproach.

Fisher frowned.

She waved one hand, pressing another one to her chest. But her coughing continued.

"Renata." Ash was up, refilling her water glass. "You're choking."

She gulped down more water and drew in a deep breath. "Fine." More coughing. Another sip and it was a little easier to breathe.

Ash squatted by her side, those gorgeous light gray eyes watching her.

Don't look at him. Bad idea. She tore her gaze from his. One more long drink of water. "I'm not choking." The words were tight and irritated. At least she wasn't choking anymore.

But Ash was still watching her. A man shouldn't be beautiful like he was.

"Really," she said, clearing her throat. The whole choking-from-near-public-humiliation thing was forgotten now—but now there was that electrified air humming between them to deal with. Last time they'd given in. This time, they had an audience.

She needed to shut out the fact that he smelled better than a fresh-out-of-the-oven gingerbread cookie and looked good enough to eat. Immediately. Her mouth went dry and every inch of her tightened with want. She cleared her throat again. "Go…eat your pie," she all but pleaded. Before her brother's spot-on twin senses picked up on something they shouldn't.

Ash smiled then—and it was one hell of a smile. "Yes, ma'am."

Even after he'd returned to his place, and his pie, she was distracted. He was distracting—all gorgeous and manly with his shirtsleeves rolled up. Even his hands were distracting. Big and strong. And oh so capable of making her experience the most incredibly intense and bone-melting sensations.

She shot a look at Kylee, then Fisher, both enjoying the conversation she was completely oblivious to. What was wrong with her? The three of them were talking about things like holidays and festivals and sharing a laugh—appropriate adult conversation. While she was thinking about Ash's hands on her body, thinking about that night. During a family dinner.

She needed to snap out of it.

"The first-place gingerbread house was devoured by the donkey that was carrying Mary to the church Christmas pageant about the same time the children's choir was struck by a stomach bug." Fisher shook his head. "Well, one kid started throwing up and it started a chain reaction. It was a sight to see. I can't guarantee we'll have that sort of excitement, but there's no shortage of entertainment," Fisher said, laughing. "You remember that?"

She nodded.

"Sounds like fun." Ash chuckled along with her brother—completely at ease the whole evening.

"That's one way to put it." Kylee was all smiles. "Where are you staying?"

"He's at the Lodge," Fisher answered for him. "I spoke with my father earlier. You don't have to eat in the guest dining room. My father, his wife, Clara, and Renata all eat in the family kitchen. The food is good and the company even better. Plus, I think you'll like my father. He's a good man. Knows everyone in town. Might be able to find you a place." He nodded. "Renata can show you where it is when you get back."

Of course I will. She used her fork to break up the remains of her pie crust.

"The place is gorgeous." Kylee was talking. "Teddy really knows how to take care of guests."

"I stayed there for my interview. You're right," Ash said, making her look at him—to find him glancing her way. "I was very well taken care of."

Did the corner of his mouth just turn up? Was he teasing her? In front of her family? Her hand tightened around her fork. A fork she really wanted to launch at his head. But that would definitely be waving a red flag in front of her brother.

But when he dared to look at her, that damnably gorgeous smile on his face, she dropped her fork. It was a quick look, but it was enough to have her melting. And seeing red. Luckily, Fisher was too busy serving more slices of Kylee's buttermilk pie to notice when she dropped her fork on the ground.

Kylee, however, saw everything.

"It was a quick trip," Fisher continued. "One night, wasn't it?"

Renata ducked, taking as long as possible to collect her fork. And hide the telltale flush burning her cheeks.

"Yep." Ash's voice was thick.

She popped up and placed her fork alongside her plate.

"Maybe it was a good thing. If you'd run into Renata, she might have talked your ear off then and you would have decided to pass on the job." Fisher chuckled.

Renata tried to laugh but it came out sounding slightly unhinged. All eyes turned her way. Enough already. She pushed her chair back and stood. Her stomach clenched, nausea settling in. After feeling queasy for a few days, the pie probably wasn't the best choice. "I should head out. I—I'm sorry." She smiled at Kylee. "Today has been…long. I'm going to head home."

Kylee pushed out of her chair. "Are you sure?"

"Sit. I'm good." Seeing Kylee move, round and awkward from her pregnancy, triggered a wave of sympathy—and guilt. "Please. I've got an early-morning meeting for the Gingerbread Festival. Finalizing judges, I hope, since Lola backed out. If you think of someone who'd be interested, let me know." She nodded, waving at Fisher, then Ash, and hurried toward the door. "Plus, I'm beat. Thanks for dinner." *And I'll make an even bigger fool of myself if I stay a minute longer.*

"You know I'm going to figure out what's going on." Fisher stood.

Her panic level continued to rise. *No. No, you're not. Please.*

Fisher hugged her, pressing a kiss to her temple. "I'll call you tomorrow."

"And I'll be busy." She smiled up at him, wishing she could sink into a nice, comforting hug. Instead, she pulled free and opened the front door. "Unless you want to judge the Gingerbread Festival?"

He held his hands up in defeat. "No. No way. 'Night then."

"'Night," she said, slipping through the door and hurrying from the front porch. Once she and her bright yellow truck were headed toward the Lodge, she could finally breathe. But, with no distractions around, it was hard to ignore the magnitude of her bizarre behavior. Instead of acting like her fun, usual self, she'd opened herself up to a boatload of questions and concerns from her brother. And his very observant wife.

But she'd never counted on Ash coming back. Ever. She might have hoped, in the beginning. Maybe even dreamed about it a few times… But now, she was over him. She was. And, if he was going to stay in town and work with her brothers, their night together needed to stay a secret. For his own safety. Not only was her twin as big as a mountain and as stubborn as a mule, he was fiercely protective.

Chapter 4

Dr. Rudolpho Santos had been her doctor since before she could remember. He'd seen her through childhood bouts of strep throat and sinus infections, sprained limbs and cracked bones—the man knew her. And she knew him. But the look on his well-wrinkled face was one she wasn't familiar with. Considering the road map of creases on his forehead, she was amazed his brows could go that high. But they did—and they were going higher by the second while he was reading her chart.

"Why?" was the question. And did she want to know the answer?

All she had to do was ask—to force the words lodged in her throat up and out and into the open. But his expression, his total silence, had her unnerved.

Before she could say a word, his dark brown eyes

met hers and he sighed heavily. A long, deep, deflating sort of sigh that didn't bode well for what was to follow. "How long has this stomach bug been bothering you, Renata?" he asked, sitting on the stool.

"A week or so now. I would have come in sooner, but it's a stomach bug—how long can that last?" She waited, the indecision on his face confusing.

"Another few months, I'd say." Those dark brown eyes searched her face.

"Months?" she asked, stunned. What kind of stomach bug was that? "Doc, I can't keep a thing down. I'm not sure I'll make it another few months—"

"That happens sometimes but you'll pull through." He broke off, his lips pressed tight.

She waited, the beginning twinges of panic setting in.

"It's not a stomach bug, Renata. You're pregnant." Another sigh. "I'm taking it this wasn't planned?"

Everything came to a screeching halt. Thoughts. Feelings. Her heart. The already frigid exam room plummeted a good twenty degrees. *What?* She blinked, hands tightening on the exam table edge. *No. No way.*

"I have to say, I'm just as surprised as you are." He flipped the paper on her chart.

I doubt that.

"I think it's best if you go see Dr. Farriday, Renata. We'll get you set up before you leave."

"Dr. Farriday?" she repeated. The same Dr. Farriday who cared for her brothers' wives. The one every pregnant woman in town went to see—because she was…pregnant.

"Healthy mothers and healthy pregnancies are her specialty." He scribbled something on her chart.

Healthy mothers. Healthy pregnancies. Pregnant? Her? No. She couldn't be.

"Dr. Santos, I'm certain there's been a mistake," she finally managed. "I can't be pregnant. It's impossible."

"Impossible?" His brows rose.

The heat in her cheeks was instantaneous. It was *possible*.

"Mmm-hmm." He nodded. "We can confirm it with a blood test."

"Yes."

He stared at her long and hard then stood. "I'll get Marcy to come in and get a blood sample." With a click of his pen and another pointed look her way, he left the exam room.

By the time Marcy returned with her little white caddy full of multicolor tipped vials, Renata was fighting back tears.

"You go on and cry," Marcy told her, patting her hand. "I cried through the first trimester with all five of my kids. And when I wasn't crying, I was eating. Got to be the size of a house every time."

Renata pressed her eyes shut and bit into her lip. There was no point in arguing with Marcy. It wasn't her fault that the test had given some sort of false positive. It wasn't her fault that Dr. Santos had acted all judgy about her supposed pregnancy. The blood test would show them all just how wrong they were. Then, she would totally expect an apology. *And* he could dig through the cabinet for one of those lollipops he gave to his younger patients.

"Sharp stick," Marcy said.

Renata didn't feel a thing. Dr. Santos's calm proclamation was still ringing in her ears. And ten minutes later, when Dr. Santos returned with his clipboard and his pen, the words were just as deafening—especially since he was saying them again.

"No mistake." He didn't look up this time. "Strong positive. Go check out with Winnie at the front and she'll help you get set up with Dr. Farriday."

"Are you sure?" she whispered, her throat constricting.

His dark eyes met hers. "One hundred percent. You are going to be a mother, Renata Boone." He paused, clicking his pen. "I'm looking forward to meeting the fellow who finally won your heart."

Oh God. Ash. John-Asher Carmichael and his charming grin and magic hands. And absolute shock and panic over seeing her again. One night. Period. That was all they'd both wanted. This. A *baby*... Her stomach flipped. This was really happening?

How was she going to tell him?

How was she going to tell her family? Her father? Anybody?

"You go see Dr. Farriday as soon as you can. It's more important than ever that you take care of yourself now, you hear me? I know it's a stressful time of year, but stress isn't good."

Did he not grasp how big a shock this was? An unplanned pregnancy sort of meant stress, didn't it? Or

was she the odd woman out? No stress? Was he kidding? Still, she nodded. Words weren't going to happen. Thankfully, numbness was sinking in.

"Winnie's waiting," he mumbled, helping her off
the table.

The walk from the exam room to the front desk took
forever. Imagination or not, it seemed like everyone in
his office already knew and was whispering about her
condition. Her only hope was that the doctor-patient
thing would prevent news of her scandal reaching her
family before she'd found the courage to tell them herself.

"Miss Boone." Winnie stressed the *Miss* with enthusiasm.

Ugh. Even better. *Winnie.* She was one of those people who lived to make others uncomfortable. And she
was very good at it. She'd recently married—again—
and this time Dr. Santos's son had been the poor fool
lined up in her sights. Since she was short on charm, her
marriage was likely the reason she now manned Dr. Santos's front desk. Maybe it was time to change doctors?

"Another Boone wedding in the mix." Winnie's
smile was hard. "I'm on hold with Dr. Farriday's office.
She's pretty full but she's trying to squeeze you in. Prenatal care is super important. For you and the baby."

Renata winced at the last sentence. Not from the
words so much as the sudden increase in volume. Almost a yell. Near enough. "I can call her later," she
offered, eager to leave—so she could fall apart in the
privacy of her truck.

Winnie shook her head. "Oh no, Dr. Santos wanted

me to make this appointment for you. Said it was essential to get you in as soon as possible." She paused, spinning her chair with the phone handset still pressed to her ear. "Oh, here, samples until Dr. Farriday can get you in." She placed a large white paper bag on the counter. "Prenatal vitamins and a little pamphlet on pregnancy." The last sentence was almost yelled.

She glared at the bag. Then Winnie.

Winnie smiled back. "Yes," she said into her phone. "Renata Boone. *R-e-n-a-t-a B-o-o-n-e*. Urinalysis and blood test were both positive." Listening. "Let me see if she's available."

She waited, trying not to look at the people seated in Dr. Santos's waiting room. With Winnie blaring the news like a town crier, there was no way any of them had missed it. No way.

Winnie listed off the date. "They have a cancellation at two."

Two days. She had no idea what her calendar looked like. Still, she nodded.

"She'll take it. Thank you." She hung up.

"Am I done?" *Please let me done.* She needed this to be over.

"You're done here. As a mother myself, I can tell you—this is only the beginning." Winnie pushed the white paper bag toward her.

As soon as she was back in her office, she threw the white paper bag in her desk and flopped into her office chair. Pregnancy had never entered her mind. Everything about that night had been so magical—almost unreal—that real-life consequences weren't part of the equation. Now… What was she going to do? Maybe the lab at Dr. Santos's was tainted somehow? But she rejected her pathetic attempt to deny the truth as soon as the thought occurred.

Like it or not, there was no way to wish this away. Her night with Ash had left lifelong consequences for her, her family and Ash, too. Unfortunately, she was the one that got to tell them her news and disappoint every single person she loved.

In order to stay busy—and away from Renata Boone—Ash had spent the next day poking around the hospital, setting up his office and driving around the county, looking for homes and exploring the region. By the time he headed to the Lodge, it was late and he was starving. With any luck, he'd raid the fridge and head to his room undetected. But there was a crowd gathered on the wraparound porch of the Lodge. A wagon strung with Christmas lights and half a dozen saddled horses waited in the side yard. Nothing like a holiday hayride.

He parked and waited, sweeping the faces of those assembled on the porch. No sign of Renata—which was good. With a deep breath, he climbed the steps to the crowded porch. Cowardly or not, the thought of fighting against the spectrum of emotions Renata caused was too much for him tonight. He slipped inside and nodded at the front desk attendant, the scents of apple cider and gingerbread making his empty stomach growl loudly. But as he crossed the great room, he caught sight of Renata, speaking to a handsome older gentleman with a commanding presence. Mr. Boone—it had to be. The family resemblance was undeniable.

Ash was trapped. A guest, a little old man pushing his walker at a snail's pace, stood in his path. No quick escape then. At this point, he wanted an escape. But the formidable expression on Mr. Boone's face gave Ash pause. And Renata? She was staring at her father like he'd sprouted a second head.

It wasn't his business. But the little old man had barely moved and Ash would have had to jump the massive leather couch to get around him.

"Renata Jean, don't give me that look," Mr. Boone was saying.

Ash looked at Renata. That was some look. Determination. Incredulity. And more than a hint of anger. And, damn, he was struck by just how beautiful she was all over again.

He stared at the old man blocking his path, willing him to pick up the pace. No luck.

"Dad…this is ridiculous." Renata's outrage had Ash turning back, watching the two—against his will.

"Your brother never calls me, worrying about you. He did this morning." His blue eyes swept over her face. "I want you to go see Doc Santos in the morning."

Her hands fisted at her sides. "I'm fine," she bit back.

Mr. Boone's brows rose. "Until I see a note from your doctor saying otherwise, you're staying out of the cold. No riding tonight." He touched her cheek. "Don't get all worked up, now. It's done. Ryder, Hunter and Eli are happy to do it. You're sick. You go on to bed."

"A doctor's note?" She laughed. "Are you kidding me?"

Ash thought of his son and the one time Curtis had come down with the flu. All the education and training in the world hadn't eased the all-consuming worry Curtis's cries had stirred in his heart. Guess that was something a father never outgrew.

Still, he understood why Renata was so surprised. She was an adult. Sick or not, she should be able to do whatever she wanted. Even if Renata's father didn't agree.

"No, ma'am. I'm not. Don't make me worry over you when I don't need to." Mr. Boone patted Renata's cheek. "Humor your old man, won't ya?"

Score one for Mr. Boone. His plea had Renata's posture easing and her expression softening. And it warmed him to see the obvious love she had for her father. Not that it was a surprise. He knew firsthand how passionate she could be. It made sense that she'd love just as fiercely.

She sighed, shaking her head. "Not like you're giving me a choice here, Daddy."

Mr. Boone chuckled. "Guess I'm not."

She rolled her eyes, but the fight was gone. Instead, Ash saw only adoration in her gaze. There was an abundance of love in this family—something he'd do well to emulate in his own household.

"Come on, now, give me a hug so I know you still love me." The older man held his arms out to Renata.

Renata didn't hesitate. She melted into her father's arms, a smile on her face. "You're so stubborn."

"Where do you think you got it from?" Mr. Boone patted her back. "You go, soak in a bath, put your feet up, read a book. Be quiet and calm, you hear?"

Over her father's shoulder, Renata's blue eyes locked with his. Her smile instantly stiffened. Her father turned, giving Ash what could only be called a head-to-toe inspection.

To walk away now would be plain rude, so he crossed the room, hand outstretched. "Mr. Boone? I'm John-Asher Carmichael. Ash. The new vet at the hospital—"

"Yes, sir. Fisher told me all about you." The man smiled instantly. "Ash. Good to meet you, son. I'd love to sit and talk a spell, but we've got this damn hayride tonight. Can I count on you to join us for breakfast in the morning?"

He'd snuck out early this morning to avoid that very thing. But there wasn't a single excuse for him to turn the man down. "If it's not an imposition?" he asked, the irritation rolling off Renata impossible to miss. The question was: Who was the irritation for? Him or her father? Both, probably.

Mr. Boone shook his head. "And call me Teddy, son. The amount of time we'll be spending together we'll practically be family."

Renata made an odd sound in the back of her throat, but when he looked her way she was staring into the fire, arms crossed over her chest.

"I appreciate the hospitality, Teddy." He smiled.

"Of course." Teddy smiled back, checked his watch and shook his head. "I'm holding everyone up. I'll see you both in the morning."

The farther away Mr. Boone got, the more Renata's smile faded.

His first thought had been escape, space, air... But now. They were both here. Alone. No time like the present to clear the air. "Renata—"

She held up her hand. "Not now."

He glanced over his shoulder, watching as Teddy Boone made his way to the front, shaking hands and making cordial small talk with guests, until he closed the door behind him. When Ash looked back, Renata was heading in the opposite direction.

Dammit.

She disappeared behind the carved wooden kitchen door on the far side of the great room. Did she want him to follow her? Or was this a not-so-subtle attempt to avoid a conversation altogether? It could wait—not like either one of them was going anywhere.

But he *was* hungry.

He followed her into the kitchen before he could stop himself—to find her rifling through the refrigerator.

"Hungry?" His stomach rumbled loud enough there was no way she could miss it. She didn't look at him. "Stomach feeling better?"

He glanced around the kitchen, impressed again. The Boones. The Lodge. The hospital. They put their full support behind things they believed in—that much was clear—down to the details. He'd noticed that during his first visit. This kitchen, with its old-fashioned wood-burning stove and its state-of-the-art range, was no different. A massive wooden banquet table lined with chairs and padded benches would sit a large crew. Perfect for the Boones. But Ash didn't sit. He was too nervous—too jumpy. Instead, he leaned against the kitchen counter and waited.

"You caught me on an off day." Finally, she glanced at him. "Maybe I thought sharing every random piece of information I know about Stonewall Crossing was riveting stuff." She smiled. "Sorry for that."

He had only fond memories of that smile. Memories he'd savored more than a few times since he'd left here. "I was… Well, I hadn't expected to see you, either, you know?" He nodded. "It was…unexpected."

Her smile grew. "Unexpected? I'm not sure that's how I would have put it. But I guess you're right."

Maybe it was being alone with him or having had the time to adjust to his presence. Whatever it was, Renata seemed like her old self. The Renata he'd taken to bed. Best to shut that line of thinking down. "I'd say that describes—" He stumbled to a stop. What was he going to say? Them? Their time together? Her? She was definitely unexpected. In the best—and worst— possible way. "My time in Stonewall Crossing so far."

Her smile faded and her eyebrows arched high. "You have no idea."

He waited. "Meaning?"

"Well… I— You…" She cleared her throat, turning her attention back to the contents of the refrigerator. "Are you hungry? Clara makes an amazing chicken pot pie." She pulled a foil-wrapped dish out and placed it on the counter, her movements awkward and jerky. Renewed tension rolled off her as she pulled two plates from the cabinet.

"Sounds good."

"Right. Coffee?" she asked, scooping a piece of pot pie onto each plate. "Or sweet tea? Water? Anything?"

"Water's fine." He cleared his throat. "We okay to talk in here?"

"Talk? Now?" She slammed the microwave with a surprising amount of force. "If you insist."

He chuckled again. What had he said to get her all fired up again? Still, now that he'd suggested it, he didn't know where to start. So he dove right in. "I'm guessing you didn't tell anyone about…us—that night."

"I did. The whole family—over breakfast the next morning." She shot him a look. "Of course not. It's no one's business. Besides, it was one night. We're adults. We can do what we want, without explanation." Her eyes locked with his. "And that night was something we both wanted."

He nodded, his throat tightening.

"And now?" She pressed her eyes shut. "My brothers wouldn't be happy if they knew. And, since you're going to be working with them—living here—it's probably best if they never know. Don't you think?" The microwave started to beep, making her jump. Her laugh was nervous.

He nodded, watching her. Brittle. Upset. Like something was right under the surface, about to break through.

"The thing is…" She drew in a deep breath. "If it does, I mean… Possibly. Come up…" She opened the microwave, pulled the plate out and offered it to him. "You'll deny it?" Was she asking him? Or herself? She turned away, putting her plate in the microwave and watching it warm.

Ash stared at her. "Is that what you want me to do?"

His personal life was his own, but he could never live a bald-faced lie. Was that what she was asking him to do? The longer she stared at the microwave, the whiter her face grew. She was scared to death. "Is my being here going to cause a problem?"

"I don't think so," she murmured, glancing at him.

Not comforting. He waited, hoping she'd say more. But she didn't. And the longer she stayed silent, the more curious he became. Fisher's comment about secrets popped up. "Seems to me your brother is on the way to figuring it out."

"Won't be too hard, soon enough," she muttered.

He set the plate on the counter. "Why do I get the feeling you're trying to tell me something?" Apprehension chewed on his gut. "You don't want to, I get that." He understood. Did he relish the idea of dealing with Fisher's anger and disapproval? Hell no. But he wasn't going to come between Renata and her family. If the last two years had taught him one thing, it was the importance of the family unit. It should be protected, treasured and nurtured. Always.

The look on her face was assessing—as if she was mulling over a problem and she was unsure of the solution. "I… I guess I'm going to just say it, okay?" She set her plate on the counter next to his and crossed her arms around her waist. But she didn't say anything. She stood there, eyes fixed on the floor, shaking.

Anticipation seeped in deep, cold and hard. Whatever she was about to say wasn't good. He'd had enough bad news to last a lifetime.

"I'm pregnant," her voice wavered, "And… I mean…

Well, it's yours." She hugged herself. "If—*if* you were wondering?" She rushed on. "But I'm not asking for anything. I'll figure this out."

He didn't hear a word of what she said next. Roaring filled his ears. Crushing, thick weight squeezed the air from his lungs and had him leaning, heavily, against the counter.

This was too much. A joke. Pregnant? No. He was just figuring out this father thing with Curtis. And now?

Renata was pregnant with his baby. His brain was processing but his body had gone cold. Until, slowly, the anxiety and tightness of her voice reached him. Her words eventually seeped in and sort of made sense. What was she saying?

"So, you know. And we'll just go on." She poked her chicken pot pie. "No one needs to know—"

What the hell? She wasn't serious. This changed everything. Everything. "Everyone will know." He stared at her stomach, imaging her round. With his baby. Breathing was impossible. "You won't be able to hide it for long. Besides, you're close with your family."

"I will figure this out," her voice wavered.

She'd said that before.

"*You'll* figure this out?" he repeated. He looked at her then—really looked at her. And what he saw hurt. The Renata he'd spent the night with had been fearless. Now…well, she was pregnant and scared to death. Fear could crush a spirit, he knew that firsthand. He didn't want that for her.

He crossed to her without thinking, prepared to offer

whatever support she needed. But she stopped him, one hand braced against his chest.

"Don't. I need to stay strong, okay?" She wouldn't look at him. "You don't need to worry. I'll be fine. I can do this."

The more she said it, the more offended he became. "I'm sure you can but that's not the way it's going to work." What the hell was he talking about? How was it going to work? He had some grand idea? Nope. He had nothing. His mind was free-falling. But *they* would come up with something. Until he had something coherent to offer, he needed to choose his words carefully. His panic was his problem, not hers. All she needed to know was he was going to be there for her. And this baby.

His baby.

Shit.

Her gaze slammed into his, startled. "Ash…" Was she trying to give him an out here? Or did she not want him around? Not that it mattered.

"What did you expect? That I'd walk away? Or, worse, pretend this baby wasn't mine?" He kept his anger in check, barely. They hadn't spent a whole lot of time together but what they had had been real—open and honest. That was how he lived life. "I won't do that."

She nodded. "I know. I thought… I was scared. I *am* scared. Okay." The fight drained out of her and, this time, she didn't resist him pulling her into his arms. It felt better then, to have her pressed against him.

He closed his eyes, battling back the images of Shanna. Curtis's pregnancy had been one nightmare after another. Her cancer had been diagnosed her first trimester. Untreatable. Incurable. From that point on, life was one long descent into misery.

"I don't know what happens next," she whispered. "What to tell people. What to do. I'm a terrible liar. Terrible."

Which was a huge comfort. "Lying is terrible. Don't do it. The truth can hurt, but it's real."

He'd learned how to lie—out of necessity. Telling Shanna everything would be okay, that he was fine, that he'd live life to the fullest, for her, every day... Whatever she needed to hear to have the peace she deserved. She'd fought hard, doing everything she could to protect her pregnancy and their son. Until her body couldn't do it anymore. Seeing his vital, fearless, dreamer of a wife turn weak and anxious had broken something inside him. He'd done his best to hide it, for her, but once those last few months had started ticking away, he'd been scared of everything. He'd known he was going to lose her and the life they'd dreamed of, and there was nothing he could do to stop that.

Renata's wavering sigh pulled him back to the present. The way her hands gripped his shirtfront constricting the vice squeezing his already fractured heart. His arms tightened around her waist out of instinct, nothing more. They were both shaken, in need of comfort—that was all this was.

They were in this together. No matter what. What he'd envisioned or wanted couldn't compete with this baby's needs. Now that was all that mattered. What was best for this baby.

Chapter 5

"You need to eat." His breath tickled her ear.

Eating would require her to let go of him and she was comfortable as she was, pressed tight against the warm, strong breadth of Ash Carmichael's chest. If she could stay like this for a few minutes longer, maybe she'd think about eating. For the first time since Dr. Santos's shocking announcement she felt better. Sure, her world was still upside down and backward, but... better.

"Renata?" His hand stroked along her back. "It'll help."

Not as much as a long, warm cuddle. She kept her mouth shut and her eyes on the ground as she stepped out of his hold.

"Eating is important for you both," he added.

Both. Meaning her baby. Their baby. The baby that was completely reliant on her. Even though this was not how she'd ever in her wildest dreams imagined things unfolding, she'd always wanted this. A baby of her own. A baby she'd shower with all the love in her heart.

Fine. She'd eat. She'd *try* to eat. Even if the flaky crust and creamy chicken held absolutely no appeal. With the tines of her fork, she rolled two peas free from the pie filling then sat the fork on the counter. "My stomach." She ran her hand along the cool surface.

"Nauseous?" he asked.

"A bit. I thought it was stress. Or lack of sleep. I never thought it was...*this*." She shrugged. "But it is." She pushed off the counter and looked at him. He was taking this remarkably well. She was not. Words jammed up in her throat, so many words.

"You'd do this on your own?" he asked. "If I wasn't here?"

She still didn't know what his being here *meant* when it came to the baby. Baby. It still sounded weird.

"Renata?" His voice was low.

Right. He had questions. "Have you met my family? I'm never on my own. Besides, how could I find you?" She cleared her throat. "*Ash* isn't a lot to go on."

He was staring at her, intent, those light gray eyes sweeping slowly over his face.

"I... I'd almost convinced myself you were a dream." Now her embarrassment was complete. "But if you didn't exist then neither would this." One hand strayed to her stomach.

His gaze followed her hand, giving her the chance

to steal a longer look at him. His jaw muscle clenched tight. Drawing attention to his very strong square jaw. How simply looking at a man could make her go soft inside was a mystery. But looking at this man did just that. His thick black lashes and oh-so-mesmerizing eyes reached deep inside her. Even now, when everything was uncertain, he inspired all sorts of tingles and aches. It was exhilarating. And, considering their present condition, ridiculous.

"It wasn't a dream." His voice was pitched low, his gaze meeting hers.

The look on his face only increased the tingles and aches. And frustration. Her wayward body was not going to take control of the conversation. It had done enough, thank you very much. "I don't know you, Ash," she started. "You don't know me."

"We'll work on that." He moved to her side, instantly rattling her. "I'm not going anywhere." His hands settled on her shoulders but she wouldn't meet his gaze. It was easier to stare at the broad expanse of his flannel-covered chest. He took a deep breath. "You're not doing this on your own. This is our baby."

It was true, but that didn't stop her from panicking. *Our baby?* He had a right to know. After that… Well, she hadn't gotten to that part yet. But now there was an "our"? What, exactly, did "our" mean?

"Renata, look at me." His voice was low and gruff.

One look in those gray eyes and she'd get even more flustered than she already was. "No."

"Why?"

Surely, he knew. He had to know. Didn't he feel this?

With him this close, thinking and moving and talking was challenging. He was just so *overwhelming*.

His voice was softer as he said, "I can think of worse things than being overwhelmingly attracted to the mother of my child."

Now he had her full attention. Her heart kicked up when their gazes collided. He did know. She wasn't the only one suffering from out-of-control want. There was no way around it—this man set her body on fire. Standing here, gazes locked and blazing, the connection shook her to the core.

He was smiling. "Why deny it? I think it's a hell of a good place to start."

She was staring at his mouth, his amazing lips, taking her mind on a detour she didn't have time to travel. "Start?" That was a whole other topic. One she did not want to add on top of the whole surprise baby thing. A little shake, gripping the cool marble counter, holding herself upright—not swaying into him. *Get a hold of yourself.*

Changing the topic. "The baby will have a family." A big, loud, interfering and loving family she didn't know how to include him in—not without the truth coming out. "We can't, shouldn't, overcomplicate this. You know? Single parenting seems to be the thing these days."

The gorgeous mouth turned down. "That's what you had in mind?"

No. "I only found out." She shook her head. "I don't have anything in mind. There hasn't been time to construct a plan or catch my breath. I've barely had time to process what's happening myself." Ten seconds ago, she was wrapped up and aching for this man. Now she was supposed to have a constructive conversation?

"Don't you think we should discuss options?" His words snapped her out of it.

"There are no *options*." Options sounded way too... emotionless. Right now, her emotions were in charge. As new and terrifying as this was, she wasn't about to give up this baby. Ever. He needed to know that up front. "About the baby?" Her voice broke. "I'm going to be a mother." She backed up, away from his distracting scent and warmth to clear her head—and into the counter to send her plate, pie and fork crashing to the floor.

"And I'm going to be a father to this baby," he said, hands on hips, looking like he meant it—even if he wasn't exactly happy about it. "While I appreciate how close you and your family are, this will be our family. And I plan to play an active part in it—to be there for you—starting now."

"Great." She bit the word out. "Perfect."

"Good."

Good wasn't the way she'd describe any of this. Telling her father and brothers was going to be hard enough without him being a part of the discussion. But he was the father. She winced. He had every right to be a part of this. Saying he wanted to be here for her, for their baby, was good? It was. So why was it hard to breathe?

Oh God. How was she going to tell her family she'd wound up pregnant from a one-night stand? It might have worked out for her brother Ryder and his wife, Annabeth, but this was different. She and Ash had no history. They were strangers. Having a baby. She covered her face, and nausea welled up all over again. "This is bad," she mumbled.

He didn't argue. Or say anything. A peek between her fingers showed him still leaning against the counter, still looking at her. Calm. Rational. Sure, his jaw looked like it could snap any moment, but overall...

"How can you be this calm?"

He tugged her hands from her face, his gaze searching. "I'm not. I promise."

Exhaustion slammed into her, hard and fast. It had been a long day. "I can barely think, let alone make decisions. Besides, I'm a list maker. This calls for lots of lists. It calms me down." She sucked in a deep breath. "If possible, it helps me sleep."

The corners of his lips dipped.

"Don't frown at me," she snapped. "You're not the one that's going to have to tell my family."

"But I will be working with your brothers daily— assuming I'll still be employed." He ran a hand over his face.

His job. Her brothers. Her stomach flipped. Again.

"There's a long road ahead of us." His attempt at confidence failed. "Telling people will be the easy part."

Every bone in her body rebelled against such an idea. "There's nothing easy about that. Not to me."

He stared up at the ceiling. "I didn't mean that." The raw anguish in his voice hurt to hear. "I have people to tell, too."

People? Ash's love life hadn't entered her mind yet

but it had been two months—he could have met someone. "It certainly complicates things in the romance department," she mumbled, forcing the words past the new lump lodged in her throat.

His gaze locked with hers, jaw clenching tight. "You're seeing someone?"

"No." She shook her head. "You just said you had *people*—"

"My son," he interrupted.

She blinked. "You have a son?" Another blink, her mind officially spinning out of control. A son? A big brother. The boy's mother? Shared custody? Was the boy there now? With Ash's ex? It was too much—all of it. Once more she was struck by just how little they knew each other. They'd been too caught up in this current between them, struck dumb by sensation and want to think beyond the time they'd shared.

He studied her for a long time. "You've gone to the doctor?"

"First official appointment is in two days." Thanks to Winnie. All she could do was hope and pray she kept it to herself. Chances were slim... Meaning she didn't have much time.

"I'll come with you."

"That's not necessary." He couldn't come with her. That would only make things worse.

She was about to argue when his phone started to ring. He pulled it from his pocket, glanced her way, then back at the phone. "Excuse me," he said, answering the call with a muffled "hello" as he walked out of the kitchen.

She stared at the kitchen door, her head hurting—on top of the swish and pitch of her stomach. Ash had had the advantage of meeting her family, staying in her home, becoming instantly immersed in her life and family. All she knew was the ridiculous effect he had on her body, that he was a veterinarian—one talented enough for her brothers to hire—and, lastly, that he had a son.

Everything else? A mystery.

Including who was on the other end of that phone call.

Ash downed his second cup of coffee and glanced at the door for the hundredth time this morning. No Renata. They'd left a hell of a lot unfinished last night and he didn't like it. Normally, he wasn't a pushy man. But nothing about this was normal. This was too big to sit by and hope things worked out. She might have run off while he was getting his nightly report from the mothers, but he knew where to find her today.

Last night had been one of the longest nights of his life. After his hunt for Renata came up empty, he'd called the mothers back and told them everything. Well…not *everything*, but enough. When'd they both peppered him with questions about who she was, her family and when they'd be getting married, Ash kept things as vague as possible. In his heart, he knew what was best for his child. A mother and a father, under one roof, sharing responsibilities and unconditional love. His father had been a hard man, sparing with his praise and affection for his son and wife. Ash had grown up looking for ways to win his father's approval, and losing him at seventeen had left a void he'd never filled. His children would never experience that. They would grow up with a loving and supportive father. If he had it his way, a family.

Now he sat, making small talk and sharing an incredible spread of homemade cinnamon rolls, fluffy scrambled eggs, crisp bacon and fresh orange juice. Teddy and his wife, Clara, were gracious hosts, eagerly sharing tidbits about the town they called home. Before he got too caught up in conversation, he got directions to the Tourism Department.

"Renata mentioned something about a Gingerbread Festival needing judges, so I thought I'd lend a hand." Not that he had the slightest interest in gingerbread houses. But if Renata was there, he would be, too.

"I'm sure she'll appreciate it," Clara said. "This time of year, her plate is always overloaded." Clara pulled another tray of cookies from the industrial oven. She'd been baking since before he joined them for breakfast. The kitchen smelled incredible. Platters were stacked high with frosted sugar-cookie Christmas trees and wreaths, gingerbread men with red-hot eyes and raisin buttons, and tins of fudge and white divinity candy. If Ash wasn't so stuffed from breakfast, he'd have eaten his fair share. "But Christmas is a special time of year and Renata likes to make sure everyone gets a healthy dose of the holiday spirit."

"She does." Teddy nodded. "But that girl needs to take care of herself. She's always finding time to watch her brothers' kids or us. What she needs to be doing is finding a good man and having her own house full of babies."

"You remind her every time you see her. Now Ash knows it, too." Clara patted his hand. "It's your fault, Teddy. You've shown your children what real love looks like. Your daughter isn't going to settle. So until the right man comes along, you'll just have to wait."

Real love. Right man. *Hell.* Whatever he offered her, he'd be asking her to settle.

Guilt, all too familiar, clawed at his stomach and set a slow throb in his temple. Renata deserved both of those things. But now the right man would also need to be willing to be a loving stepfather to her baby. *Their* baby. His hands were unsteady as they spun the coffee cup he held, the surface of the black liquid rippling. *His* baby. A baby he wanted to raise—not some mystery man that might come along and sweep Renata off her feet. The guilt twisted into something heavier, hotter—and bitter. Anger.

At who? The only person he had a right to be angry with was himself—for being foolish enough to wind up in this position.

"Well, he needs to hurry up already." Teddy kept on, chuckling. "She wants a child and husband and a spot on the vow tree." He sighed.

"What's the vow tree?" He glanced up from his coffee.

Clara nudged Teddy.

"It's a Boone tradition," Teddy explained, waving any true explanation aside.

"Meaning it's a secret—unless you're a Boone."

Clara winked. "An incredibly special and romantic secret." With a kiss to Teddy Boone's forehead, she added, "Now, stop worrying over your daughter. She'd tell you to mind your own business and give you one of her 'I can take care of myself' looks."

Ash could imagine that look.

Teddy patted his wife's arm. "You're right, as always. Besides, there isn't a man alive that deserves her. And that's the truth." He winked at Ash.

He tried like hell to smile in return.

Would Teddy Boone approve of him as his son-in-law? As much as he hoped so, he had his doubts. Teddy was an old-fashioned man with old-fashioned values. Having a pregnant, unmarried daughter would be a hard pill for Mr. Boone to swallow. Teddy Boone would not be happy—over any of this—but he'd understand, if not approve, when Ash proposed to Renata. At least, he sure as hell hoped so. He'd spent most of the night trying to come up with solutions that made sense. None did—except one. Marrying Renata. Not because she needed him—she'd made it clear she didn't—but because it was best for the baby.

"She seems to love her work," he offered. "About talked my ear off at Fisher's place the other night."

Teddy chuckled. "She does, indeed. No doubt about that. A real hard worker, too." He sipped his coffee.

"Like her father. And brothers." Clara refilled his coffee cup. "Ash, when you stop by Renata's office, you could drop in at the real estate office a few blocks away. With any luck, there might be something good listed."

Conversation wandered into what he was looking for.

When Curtis came up, Teddy and Clara had only the best things to say about the local schools—grandparents through and through. His mother and Betty would fit in just fine here.

Ash gulped down the rest of his black coffee and stood. "Guess I'll head that way. Thank you, again, for breakfast."

With a wave, Ash headed out and climbed into his truck, resolve surging through his veins. Things were starting off rough, no denying that, but Ash would do his damnedest to smooth things over as soon as possible. Hopefully now, after a good night's rest, Renata would be more willing to sit down and develop a plan for how to move forward.

On impulse, he stopped at a small floral shop and bought a bouquet of flowers. A peace offering couldn't hurt. Once he parked, he smoothed his shirt, grabbed the flowers and walked into the City Offices—one of which was the Tourism Department.

A middle-aged woman looked up from her desk, eyes peeking over her reading glasses. "Good morning. Can I help you?"

"I hope so. I'm looking for Renata Boone." He tried for a charming smile.

She caught sight of the flowers, her eyes going owl-like. "Miss Boone?"

He nodded.

Not a blink. "Is she expecting you?"

"No." He looked pointedly at the flowers. "I was hoping to surprise her." *And convince her to marry me.*

The woman's expression went from cautious to excited. "Oh, I bet she will be. You go on. Her office is at the end of the hall, to the right."

Ash nodded his thanks, walked down the hall and knocked on Renata's door. Her muffled "Come in," was the only invitation he needed.

"Irma," Renata said, not looking up from the papers spread across her desk. "Have we heard back about the portable stage yet? I don't know what we'll do if the school doesn't have it."

"I can go ask her if you like," he offered, closing the office door behind him.

"Ash…" She stood. "I didn't expect you." He could see that. "Why are you here?"

Sometimes he forgot just how beautiful she was. Like now. He was too tongue-tied to say a damn thing, so he offered her the flowers. The whole charming thing was going to be a challenge.

"Flowers?" She couldn't have been more surprised.

And cute. "A man's been known to bring a woman flowers now and then." He chuckled.

Her cheeks turned a lovely shade of pink. "I—I… Thank you." She took the flowers, staring down at the blooms as she asked, "You stopped by to give me flowers?"

He sat. "Partly. Thought I'd sign up to judge your Gingerbread Festival."

Her eyes locked with his. Surprise, again. Good. The element of surprise would keep her on her toes and give him the upper hand.

But as she sank into her seat, she looked his way with open suspicion. "Why?"

"It'll give us time together." He saw no point in beating around the bush.

Her shoulders drooped. "Ash, you don't need to do this—"

"Maybe I want to." Their futures were forever tied now. They owed it to each other—and their baby—to get to know one another.

She looked at him then, those blue eyes knocking the air from his lungs. He waited, bracing himself for what she'd say or do next. But when she finally spoke, she neatly sidestepped the elephant in the room altogether. "Have you ever judged a baking competition before? Or a gingerbread house competition?"

"No. But I've eaten my fair share." He grinned, watching her do her best to fight back an answering smile.

She shook her head, losing her battle in spite of her best efforts. "You go ahead and tease all you want, but this is a serious competition."

She looked tired. Like she hadn't slept all that well last night. He knew the feeling. Teddy Boone was right. She had to start taking better care of herself—for the baby's sake if nothing else. "Did you eat breakfast?" he asked.

He caught her glance at the clock on her wall. "I wasn't hungry. But I'll have a big lunch to make up for it."

"I'm headed to the real estate place around the corner." He stood. "I'll come back to get you and we can have lunch together."

"Wait," she said, placing the flowers on her desk and standing. "I can't have lunch today. I'm too busy."

He didn't doubt she was busy but, dammit, he wasn't a fool. She was doing her best to keep him at arm's length. Guess she needed to know he could be just as stubborn as she was.

"You have to eat. Besides, how else are you going to catch me up to speed on the whole judging thing? You just said it was a *serious competition.* I don't want to mess that up for anyone."

She wavered, chewing on her lower lip. That was the thing about Renata—that mix of genuine sweetness and mind-numbing sexiness. He had to focus, to keep his goal in mind, or he'd be staring at her like an idiot in no time. Again. "Be back at eleven—since you didn't eat breakfast," he reminded her. "The baby's growing, Renata. It's up to you to take care of the both of you."

"Ash," she squeaked. Her eyes widened and the color drained from her cheeks as she marched around the desk and opened her office door. "I can take care of me...us...just fine." Her defiant whisper was the cutest damn thing he'd ever seen.

He nodded, standing in the doorway—inches from her. "Good, glad to hear it. Eleven it is." She smelled like roses.

"Ash," she hissed when he turned to go.

He faced her, close enough to breathe her in—and make the air between them spark instantly to life. And it did. Every inch of him was aware of one thing. "Renata," he murmured, the urge to touch her crowding in on him.

She was breathing heavily, her cheeks resuming that rosy glow. "You… I…"

Damn it all, he couldn't help himself. His fingertips traced along her satin skin. Her temple, down her cheek, along her jaw, to her chin. "You're glad I stopped by. Can't wait for lunch?" He paused, smiling. "Really want a kiss goodbye?"

She shook her head, her gaze fixed on his mouth. Her lips parted slightly.

Well hell. *He* wanted to kiss her goodbye. Wanted to feel her in his arms. More than wanted to. "*Need* a kiss goodbye?" He could barely get the words out.

She shook her head again but didn't move when he leaned in. It would be easy to pull her close. She wouldn't resist—he knew it. If they weren't in her office, he might have considered it. But he wasn't sure pressing her flat against a wall to kiss her senseless was the same thing as being charming. And he needed to be charming. He dug deep, resisting what he wanted for what needed to be done. Almost. At the last minute, he kissed her cheek.

Hearing her soft sound of disappointment and annoyance had him smiling the rest of the morning.

Chapter 6

Renata was mortified. As a result, she'd spent the past few hours in hiding in her office with the door closed. Never in her life had she behaved so...so unprofessionally.

Not that it was her fault.

He'd kissed *her.* What had he been thinking?

He'd kissed her and Irma *saw* him—saw the whole thing. She'd probably even seen the crushing disappointment Renata felt when he'd kissed only her cheek.

But it wasn't just Irma. No, right as Ash was walking away, the city manager—and her office neighbor—Quinton Sheehan had walked out. She'd had no choice but to introduce them. And Quinton, being Quinton, had spent another thirty minutes chatting Ash up. Before it was all done, Irma had made the men coffee and the three of them had lingered outside her office, laughing and talking like old friends while she'd tried to get some work done.

When he'd finally left, she'd stopped pretending to be engrossed in the open spreadsheet on her monitor and stared blindly at the wall in front of her. What had just happened? He'd brought her flowers. Flowers? *And* volunteered to judge the Gingerbread Festival? He had no idea he'd saved her a big headache by filling a spot most locals didn't want to touch with a ten-foot pole.

But why? To spend time with her? He didn't need to do that. She'd made it perfectly clear she had no expectations of him. Hadn't she? Last night was a blur. She remembered babbling, again, and holding on to him for dear life—hardly her finest moment. But she had told him she had no expectations of him. That included bringing her flowers. Or judging the Gingerbread Festival.

He'd only mentioned the baby once. Even then, it had been offhanded. A complete turnaround from all his intensity and determination of last night.

"Maybe he just likes to drive me crazy," she murmured, deciding the best thing to do was not think about him, for now. Her inbox grew with each passing second and she had a dozen or more phone calls to return. Forgetting Ash was the only chance she had of getting any work done.

But the gorgeous bouquet of pink roses and white hydrangea flooded her office with a heavenly scent—and kept his dark-haired, light-eyed, devilishly handsome face foremost in her mind.

Enough. Eleven o'clock would be here before she

knew it. Not that she'd actually *agreed* to have lunch with him, had she? No, she hadn't. But that wouldn't stop him from showing up. She smiled, doing her best to focus on her endless to-do list.

There wasn't time to put off the final touches on her brother Archer's Christmas Benefit Ball for his horse refuge. The annual budget meeting was next week. And going over the state's tourism bus tour route revisions meant an hour of explanations when it came to city council. She needed to have answers ready. Which meant time, research and actual work. Not getting hot and bothered over Ash Carmichael.

Irma was no help. Every twenty minutes or so, she'd pop in to offer her a cup of coffee or a water bottle. Each time, Irma slipped in some question or compliment about Ash. And how thoughtful his flowers were. Renata's repeated assurances that Ash was only a friend were blatantly ignored. Even Quinton sounded off, from his open office, that he seemed like a fine addition to the town.

She pressed her hand against her stomach, still vaguely nauseous, once more mulling over his bizarre behavior this morning.

She managed to confirm the big band and double-check on the special menu items the caterer was preparing for the Christmas Benefit Ball. Poor Archer was clueless when it came to social affairs. And, if she was being honest, his people skills needed work, too, so Renata had offered to help where she could. She drew a red line through the items on her to-do list. *Only nine hundred and ninety-nine more things to go.*

The mobile stage had been located in the agriculture barn of the high school. The coach had volunteered to bring it over Friday. Another check.

A quick glance at the clock told her it was ten after eleven. Ash was late.

She should be relieved. Not disappointed. No, she wasn't disappointed.

But she was hungry.

If she was lucky, she'd leave before Ash arrived. She grabbed her coat, slipped it on, closed her office and hurried down the hall. "Irma, I'm going to lunch—"

Ash opened the front door. "Ready and waiting?" He was all smiles.

Irma giggled. "You two have a nice lunch, now."

Renata bit back a curse.

"We will," Ash assured her.

Did he just wink at Irma? Really? She didn't say a word as she brushed past him and onto the porch of the City Offices. A gust of wind slammed into her.

"Here," he said, pulling her arm through his.

She glared up at him. "That's not necessary."

"Being a gentleman?" He frowned down at her. "It is where I'm from."

"Where would that be?" One more thing she didn't know about him.

"Ada, Oklahoma." He smiled. "Small place. Good people."

Lips pressed tight, she let him lead her down the street. Pop's Bakery. She froze. "Somewhere else?" she asked, her voice tight. They could not be seen there. Lola Stephens was a dear but there was no bigger gossip in Stonewall Crossing. She'd light up like a Christmas tree over Ash Carmichael and want to know every little thing about him—including why they were having lunch together.

He kept going, taking hold of the door handle. "Your dad said this place was incredible," Ash said. "No good?"

"It's good." But she wouldn't budge.

"Then we should go in. Where it's warmer. And there's food. Since you didn't eat this morning." He paused. "And the baby—"

"Stop. Now. Ash," she cut him off, looking over her shoulder, brushing past him into Pop's Bakery.

Ash was chuckling, damn him.

"Renata, good to see you, young lady." Carl Stephens, the owner of Pop's Bakery, gave her a firm hug. "Out and about in this cold?"

"I was hungry. A little cold won't stop me from eating your delicious cooking." She smiled. "Besides, I had to bring our newest resident by. Carl Stephens, this is Ash Carmichael, the new veterinarian out at the university's veterinary hospital."

"Nice to meet you." Carl shook his hand. "Can't think of a better tour guide than Renata."

"All part of the job." She hoped that would end any further speculation Carl and his wife, Lola, might make about the pair. She knew better, but she still hoped.

"Let's get you two fed." Carl led them to a table in the middle of the room.

Considering there were plenty of other tables in far

less prominent locations, she was tempted to ask for another one. But Ash was pulling a chair out for her.

"This is great," Ash said.

Damn, if he wasn't charming. His dark wind-blown hair, strong jaw and ruddy cheeks. And that smile. Her heart thumped—as if she needed further proof that she had no immunity to this man. She sat.

"Is that deer wearing a Christmas hat?" Ash asked, pointing to one of Carl's annual decorations: a taxidermy head mount of a whitetail deer—decked out with a Santa hat and blinking Christmas lights.

"It is. Folk around these parts sort of expect it this time of year. Guess I do, too. Wouldn't be Christmas without it." Carl nodded. "You two look over the menus while I get Lola. If I let you leave without meeting her, I'll be in the doghouse for a week." Carl winked and disappeared into the back.

"You look ready to bolt," Ash murmured.

"Lola Stephens is the loudest, nosiest busybody in town," Renata whispered, leaning across the table. "Do not mention a thing about…well, you know what."

He leaned forward. "My judging the Gingerbread Festival? Or the baby?" Ash whispered back, eyes sparkling. "Why did you want to eat here then?"

He was teasing her now? Grinning like that? "Ash Carmichael." Her voice was shaking. "You are, without a doubt—"

"Wishing I'd kissed you proper before I left this morning?" he finished. "I am. I've been regretting it all morning."

Renata was speechless, again. She was never speechless. Ever. But any attempt at a witty comeback fizzled out. Those gray eyes burned so hot her body shuddered from the heat. Which would be fine if they weren't where they were… With Lola Stephens standing by their table, watching the two of them, all wide-eyed and with an even wider grin.

This is bad.

"Lola." She sat back quickly, hoping the older woman hadn't heard him. That would be so bad.

"I was waiting for one of you to see me." She was delighted. Just delighted.

This was very bad.

Ash was on his feet. "You must be Lola Stephens? Clara said I had to meet you while I was in town."

"She did?" Lola smiled.

"Ash Carmichael," he said, taking her hand in his. "It's a pleasure, ma'am."

"Oh, poo, sugar. The pleasure is all mine." Lola Stephens was blushing. Because Ash Carmichael was good. "Sit down, please. Now, why did Clara say you needed to meet me?"

"If anyone knew of a place for sale, you'd probably have heard about it. She also said I needed to have one of your husband's raspberry tarts, if there are any."

"He's the new veterinarian, Lola," Carl filled in.

"Oh, that's wonderful," Lola said, glancing back and forth between them. "You're staying in Stonewall Crossing? And looking for a home. A family home? Or more of a bachelor pad?"

Renata wanted to kick him under the table when he

looked her way. It wasn't just any look—it was loaded with all sorts of meaning.

"Family," Ash answered, his gaze falling from hers. "I have a son. He's busy—the sort of busy that needs room to run and play and grow."

What was his name? Did Ash's son look like him? Or his mother? Chances were, he was adorable. He was half Ash, after all.

"Oh, I see." Lola's smile dimmed. "And when will Mrs. Carmichael be joining us?"

Considering the context of the conversation, it didn't sound invasive. Except Renata knew Lola Stephens. She had a heart of gold, helping everyone who needed it—while collecting and distributing all the little bits and pieces of information she regularly collected. Like now. Ash Carmichael was a mystery and Lola was about to get the inside scoop on the town's newest resident.

"My wife passed when my son was born," he said.

With that sentence, the world fell away. Pain reached inside her chest and squeezed her heart, the edge to his voice slicing deep. If ever there was a reason for a person to hurt, this was it. And there was no denying the pain in his eyes, no matter how hard he tried to hide it. "Ash, I'm so sorry," Renata murmured, devastated on his behalf. "I had no idea."

"I don't talk about it." His gaze found hers, the haunted torment she glimpsed gutting her. "Tends to make people feel bad. And for long awkward silences. Like now."

He was doing his best to be blasé, but she saw through it. And she longed to reach for him. His hand lay there, on the table—close enough to touch. It seemed like the right thing to do. Covering his large hand with her own out of sympathy. It was the human thing to do, surely? His hand turned, catching hers and squeezing gently. How could she let go then? When he held on to her?

"It's just me and Curtis, for now." His chuckle was forced. "My mother-in-law and mother have been taking care of him and helping out whenever I need. Like now."

"Sound like good folk," Lola said. "Family matters."

"Yes, ma'am. Nothing is more important." His gray eyes fixed on her. "Family is all that matters."

"When will they be joining you?" Lola asked.

"Tonight," he answered, smiling. "It'll be good to have him with me."

Tonight she'd meet Ash's son. Tonight she'd meet the boy that would be her baby's big brother. And she couldn't wait to meet him. "At the Lodge?" she asked.

He nodded.

"Well now, tragedy strikes at all ages. You're young, son," Carl spoke up. "Good-looking and, if you were hired at the university, hardworking and sharp. You keep your heart open and you'll find love again." He draped his arm around Lola's shoulder.

Lola was watching them again, like a hawk. But the hurt in Ash's eyes had Renata holding on to Ash's hand until their food arrived.

Ash pushed aside his empty plate and sat back, offering Lola Stephens a smile as she placed his dessert in front of him.

"Hope it lives up to Clara's praise. You sure you don't

want anything, Renata? You barely touched your food."
Lola tsked. "Sugar, you need to eat something or you're
going to waste away. We wouldn't want that, would we,
Dr. Carmichael?"

"No, ma'am," he agreed, moving the napkin dis-
penser from the middle of the table and pushing the plate
into the middle. "Maybe we can get another spoon?"
he asked.

Lola winked and hurried across the diner. But when
he looked at Renata, she was glaring at him—blue
eyes blazing.

"Don't like your salad?" He'd watched her poke
through the strawberry, chicken and spinach salad for
the last forty minutes.

With a sigh, she mumbled, "My stomach has been
a little unpredictable recently, Dr. Carmichael." One
brow arched high.

"Your father said this was the most stressful time
of the year for you. Stress can take a physical toll on
the body," he suggested. "Not to mention it's not good
for a pregnancy—"

"What else did my father tell you?" she cut him off,
eyes narrowed.

"A bunch." He smiled, taking a large bite of tart. "He
worries you'll move to Fire Gorge now that your best
friends are there? Worries you take on too much for
others. He wants you to settle down and have a family.
He wants you to take care of yourself. Said something
about the vow tree?"

She choked on her water. "He mentioned the vow
tree?"

"Some family secret I gather?" He waited, hoping she'd elaborate.

"Which is why I'm surprised." Her long blond hair moved in time with the shaking of her head. Her coloring was off. A little pale. A little green.

"It'll get easier further along. The nausea, I mean." He paused. "Which reminds me, I wanted to talk to you." The instant stiffening of her spine reminded him to keep it light.

"We're not talking here," she whispered. "Ash, please, Lola probably has the table bugged and hidden cameras all around this place. You have no idea…" Then those blue eyes blazed a little brighter at his smile.

Teddy and Clara had recommended the raspberry tarts—but they'd told him all about Lola Stephens and her predilection for gossip. He needed Renata to listen, without arguing. Pop's Bakery seemed like the perfect place to do just that.

"Maybe you do. Why, exactly, are we here?" She sat back, crossing her arms over her stomach.

"Clara told me about the tarts." He spooned a mouthful of the powdered-sugar-topped confection into his mouth. The flavor erupted on his tongue, buttery sweetness that he would have been able to enjoy a little more if Renata wasn't shooting daggers his way.

"Here you go." Lola placed the spoon on the table, her eyes sweeping over them both before she headed back to her place at the counter.

"I'm sure Clara also told you Lola knows everything about everybody? That her favorite pastime is sticking her nose into other people's business. Nicely, but nosy all the same." Her blue gaze darted over his shoulder "It's no accident that she's now stationed herself at the cash register. I don't know what you're after, Ash, but why don't you cut to the chase?"

She was sincerely upset—something he'd wanted to avoid. But there was no help for it. Might as well be direct. "Did you sleep last night?"

Her fingers wrapped around the spoon handle and Ash pushed the plate closer to her. "No." She took a small spoonful of the tart.

"Neither did I."

One bite tempted her to lean forward for another spoonful.

"There's no easy solution here, Renata. We both know that." He paused long enough for her to nod before he went on. "In fact, as far as I can tell, there's only one solution."

She took another bite of tart. "By all means, share."

"You were right when you said we don't know each other well. What I do know, I like."

Her gaze drifted from the tart to his face. "Agreed." Red stained her cheeks before her gaze returned to the tart.

"We need to decide what's best for the baby." He intentionally lowered his voice, leaning forward for another spoonful.

Her spoon clattered to the tabletop and she kicked him under the table.

He frowned and rubbed his calf. "*That* won't draw attention."

"I'm pretty sure it's too late to avoid that," she snapped back.

"Then I guess it won't matter if I get down on one knee to ask what I'm going to ask?" He set his spoon down, searching those blue eyes for even the tiniest sliver of encouragement.

"You spend breakfast talking to my father and decide to...to... You do realize what year it is, right?" She hugged herself. "I mean, I know my dad's charming and all, but you cannot be serious, Ash?"

"About marrying you?" He nodded. "Absolutely. It's best for the baby." Her kick was a bit harder this time. Only saving grace? She wasn't wearing her cowboy boots.

"Sorry," she mumbled, appearing just as startled as he was. "Involuntary reflex that time."

"What's best is two parents. A family. Under the same roof. Stability. Being there for each other, no matter what."

"And love?" she asked, her voice going up an octave. "What about that?"

"I love my son." He frowned. "I will love this child, too. Deeply."

Her gaze fell away. "That's not what I was talking about."

Everything Teddy had said this morning—love and family and the right man—burned a hole in the middle of his forehead. Words clogged his throat. "I know."

Seconds ticked by, long enough for her to glance his way. "Exactly."

"You said it. We don't know each other yet—"

"For all you know, we'll end up...hating each other.

And what about your son? What if he doesn't like me? Or… I'm a terrible mother." She shook her head. "Not that I'll be a terrible mother. I'll be an amazing mother—with or without a husband. This isn't a solution, it's taking a difficult situation and making it ten times worse." Her eyes were blazing and her nose wrinkled in frustration.

He couldn't imagine hating Renata Boone or how marrying her could make this worse—but now wasn't the time to argue. Or to point out that the very fiber of his being rebelled at the possibility of another man parenting his child. From the set of her jaw to her ramrod posture, he could tell he was losing this argument. "Maybe take some time to think about it."

He hated the sheen that filled her blue eyes.

"I don't need to think about it, John-Asher Carmichael." All the color drained from her face. "Marrying you isn't an option."

Her reaction surprised him. More than that, it was one hell of a knock to the ego. He hadn't expected her to light up like a kid on Christmas morning or anything but she was acting like he'd insulted her.

"And your family? You think they'll agree with that answer?" He tapped his fingers on the table. "This isn't just me and you we're talking about—"

She bolted to her feet. "Oh—ah—um," she stammered. "I'm so sorry. I forgot. An appointment. With… someone." Her mouth opened, then closed, before she headed toward the door, tripping on one chair leg but managing to slip from the restaurant before he could reach her.

"Everything okay, son?" Carl Stephens appeared. "I've known that girl a long time and I've never seen her worked up like that before."

Ash stared blindly out the large picture window that took up the front of the bakery. There had been no hesitation—no room for negotiation. She'd turned him down flat and walked away. What the hell had he expected? She was right. They were strangers. No, not strangers. Not after the night they'd spent together. And now, this baby? This baby deserved more than a knee-jerk reaction and a rapid dismissal.

"Son?" Carl repeated, sharper this time. There was no denying the suspicion on the man's face—or the disapproval in his tone.

"I'm out of practice, I guess." He shrugged, shooting for humor. "Need to up my charm. Or something."

Carl Stephens chuckled. "Damn but that woman gets it right every time."

Ash frowned. "Sorry?"

"My wife." The older man clapped him on the shoulder. "She said she saw something between you two the minute you walked in. Don't give up hope. My wife swears that little lady you were having lunch with is sweet on you." He sighed. "Lola's never wrong—something she never lets me forget."

As much as Ash wanted to believe Lola Stephens's intuition, he knew better. If Lola was never wrong, Renata wouldn't have been so quick to turn him down.

Chapter 7

Family dinner meant extra tables and chairs to accommodate her brothers, their wives and all their offspring. She enjoyed the chaos and noise and overlapping conversations that lasted through dessert. The happiness on her father's face filled her with love. That was what family should be. Loud and unpredictable, messy and invasive, heartache and the occasional squabble—but, always, love. Why didn't Ash get that?

The pain he still felt over losing his wife spoke volumes. He'd loved her. Renata wanted that. No, she deserved that. Marrying a man who didn't love her, who didn't light up when he saw her, was unfathomable.

Baby or no baby.

Instead of dwelling on Ash and his ridiculous behavior, she put a roll on each plate, butter and honey on the table, and made sure there was an abundance of extra napkins. All was well, until Clara pulled the turkey from the oven. Something about the aroma of all that golden-brown deliciousness had her unobtrusively hurrying to the closest bathroom.

She washed her face and hands, ran a cool cloth along the back of her neck and stared at her reflection. "We've got to work on this throwing up thing," she murmured, pressing her hand to her stomach. "Clara's turkey is delicious." She sucked in a deep breath, smoothed her hair behind her ears and went back to poke at her food.

But Fisher was waiting for her in the great room—wearing no less than a scowl. He'd been out of sorts all afternoon, sullen and quiet. He was acting more like Archer than her easy-to-laugh twin.

"What's wrong?" she asked. Her bear of a brother was a gentle giant, for the most part. But when something riled him up, his temper was a force to be reckoned with. He looked plenty riled up at the moment. "You look upset."

"I am." He crossed his arms over his chest and glared down at her. "I ran into Winnie this morning."

Her mind screeched to a stop.

"You know she's working at Dr. Santos's clinic now?" His words were low and gruff.

She knew. Damn it all. That woman. That horrible, nasty woman. The floor seemed to wave and buckle beneath her feet. The harder her brother looked at her, the worse it got. "Is she?" Why was the room so cold? And airless? "I mean, yes."

"You know she is." His hands settled on her shoulders, steadying her. His blue eyes—so like hers—assessing. "Renata... Don't you have something to tell me? Us? All of us?"

Not yet. Not now. Life had been going ninety miles an hour for the last forty-eight hours. Before she dumped this on her family, she needed Ash to let go of this marriage foolishness. "No," she whispered, knowing good and well her twin would see through her pathetic attempt at a lie.

"Renata Jean." He crossed his arms over his broad chest and waited.

"Did you really just use my middle name? You're not Dad, Fisher. This is my business."

"Are you kidding me?" His face was beet red. "I'm your brother. Your twin. *You* are my business."

Part of her had never loved her brother as much as she did at that moment. But another part of her needed him to lower his voice and respect her privacy. Now.

"What's all the yelling about?" Hunter walked out of the kitchen. He took his role as the eldest sibling seriously, doing his best to keep his brothers and sister in line.

"Nothing," she answered. *Too late now.*

"Oh, it's something all right," Fisher argued—infuriating her further.

He had no right to do this. *She'd* tell her family when she was ready. And, right now, she was not ready. "Fisher. Stop!"

Archer and Ryder pushed through the door next.

"We can hear you in the kitchen," Ryder said, teasing. "You guys give me grief about setting an example for the kids, but I've never had a yelling match during a family dinner."

Neither she nor Fisher smiled. It took a lot to make her twin lose his temper. He was close now.

"What's happening?" Archer's ever-analytical gaze swung between Fisher and Renata.

"Nothing," she snapped. "For once in my life, respect my privacy. Without interfering or doing what you think is best for me."

"Renata." Fisher's anger gave way to something a hundred times worse. His gaze fell from hers, his shoulders slumping in defeat. "You can't expect me to stop trying to protect you now? Not when it's always been my job. I can't stand by and let you get hurt." He took her hand in his.

"Get hurt? What the hell's going on?" Now Ryder was up in arms, his voice hardening. "Whose ass are we kicking?"

"That's what we're trying to figure out." Hunter was staring at her.

They were all staring at her.

And now her father was headed their way. "What is going on out here? Food's on the table. Clara and Eden made some mighty fine-looking fried chicken. Josie made that potato salad I love. And Kylee made a buttermilk pie." He frowned. "Who's doing all the yelling and why?"

Renata held her breath, hoping, praying—

"These two," Archer said, pointing between Renata and Fisher.

"We're fine," she argued. "Let's go back and eat together."

"I like that idea," her father agreed, hooking her arm through his and patting her hand.

"You sure you won't be running back to the bathroom again?" Fisher asked, scowling again.

Renata stared at him, silently pleading him to stop.

He shook his head then, refusing to look at her. "Kylee always has it really bad at the beginning of the pregnancy, too. But, the further along you get, the less morning sickness you'll have. Hopefully."

Renata was speechless. Fisher had outed her. In front of her brothers. And her father. Until now, he'd always been on her side. Always.

The room was absolutely quiet. And still. Like they were all suspended in space—waiting for the other to make the first move. Renata would be perfectly happy if a hole opened up in the floor and swallowed her.

But things only got worse when Ash walked in, an adorable dark-haired toddler on his hip, smiling a sweet baby grin. Two middle-aged women followed in his wake.

"Can we move this some place more private?" she hissed, desperation mounting.

"You're pregnant?" Archer looked stunned. And he was talking way too loudly.

Because now Ash and the women were looking their way, too.

"Are you… Who… What the hell?" Ryder growled. "Like I said, whose ass are we kicking?"

She was doing her best not to stare at Ash, but the

look of sheer determination and resignation on his face set off warning bells. He straightened, heading straight toward them. And it took everything she had not to run from the room. Nope, no running away. It's not like this could get worse. She was shaking her head, holding up her hands, before she realized what she was doing.

Her brothers and father, all frowning and confused, looked from her to Ash, then back again.

"Everything okay?" Ash was looking at her, his voice low and soothing.

"Fine, Dr. Carmichael," Archer snapped. He wasn't a fan of outsiders butting in. Ever.

"This is a family matter, Ash." Fisher's smile was brittle—not in the least bit welcoming.

Still, Ash was looking at her, not her brothers or her father or the women standing, gawking, behind him. The toddler Ash carried turned huge eyes on the crowd assembled, making baby sounds, repeating, "Hi," and waving frantically.

She couldn't help it, she waved back. He, Ash's son, was beautiful. "Curtis?" she asked.

Ash nodded.

Curtis clapped his hands and looked up at Ash, all the love in the world on his little face. "Daddy here."

Ash nodded and pressed a kiss to the boy's forehead. "I wanted to be here when you did this."

She winced, pressing her eyes shut. Yes. Apparently, it could get worse.

Ryder was on the verge. "Why would she—"

"You're kidding me?" Fisher groaned, long and loud. "It's yours? It's his."

"He's been here what? A week? Days?" Archer shot Fisher a look of pure irritation.

"He was here in October." Hunter glanced her way. "For the interview."

Her brothers turned on Ash, wound tight and stone-faced. This was very bad.

"Well," her father mumbled, giving Ash a look Renata had never seen before. Still, his expression softened when Curtis waved at him. Her father adored children, especially his grandchildren. "Is that the way of it?" he asked.

She nodded again.

Her father was patting her arm again. "I see."

He didn't see. But she needed him to, before anyone jumped ahead and started presuming what happened next. "Ash and I will co-parent. We've agreed that's best."

"What the hell does that mean?" Ryder asked, his jaw locked stiff and his hands fisting at his sides.

"It means we will raise this baby together—"

"Of course you will," her father agreed, his spirits lifting. "Ash here is a solid young man. He knows what the right thing to do is, given the situation."

"We're not getting married, Dad." Her tone was firm. But the announcement was met with instant protest. Loudly. With curses. And all sorts of threatening looks Ash's way. It horrified her to realize poor Ash's safety was guaranteed only because his son was in his arms. His son, who burst into tears from the hostility and tension radiating off her beloved family. Ash started bouncing the boy, one hand patting his back.

It was oddly comforting to her—the calm efficiency of Ash's actions.

"Stop it." She'd never lost her temper or dared to raise her voice to her family. But now, well, they'd have to accept her decision because it was her decision. "Whether or not you like this doesn't matter. This is between Ash and me. I love how much you all love me. But I know what's best for me. I won't settle in my marriage—I can't. And if you do or say anything to bully Ash, I will never forgive you. Ever. Understood?" She stared each of her brothers down. "I mean it."

One by one their gazes fell away, the tension in the air dropping a few notches. It was something. She meant what she'd said and they knew it.

But the sadness on her father's face… Her heart clamped down hard and tore wide, sharp and jagged enough to knock the air from her lungs. She was the cause of that. "I'm sorry, Dad." It hurt to say the words.

He cleared his throat. "If this is what you and Ash feel is best, I'm sure you know what you're doing."

Ryder made a sound that resembled a snort but didn't say a word.

"No, now, I mean it," her father said, patting her cheek. "I trust you, girl. Do what's in your heart."

Her eyes were burning and her throat was too tight to say a word, so she nodded.

"I expect we'll be seeing a lot of you." Her father turned to Ash then, avoiding his gaze to smile at Curtis. "This your boy? He's a handsome fella."

"Thank you." Ash didn't look happy. At all. And it worried her. If her family learned he was willing to propose… He was right. They'd side with him. And then what? She needed her family on her side—the right side—not the side where she married a man who didn't love her. "And this is my mother and my mother-in-law. They'll be moving here with me."

Another new piece of information. Not that it mattered. She'd set everyone straight.

Renata was vaguely aware of the introductions. Her father was, as always, gracious and charming. If he was struggling to accept her life-altering news, there was no evidence of it. Instead, he escorted Ash and his family back to the desk to help them check in. Even though she felt Ash's gaze on her, she avoided his eyes.

"I don't keep things from Josie," Hunter said, hugging her.

"No, I'd never ask that of you. But I'd appreciate it if we could keep it in the family—for now." She shrugged.

"Considering where I found out, don't you think that's a little unlikely?" Fisher asked. "She didn't come straight out with it, mind you. But there was no misunderstanding what her meaning was. In the middle of Pop's, too."

Which was disheartening. Since she'd found out she was pregnant, she'd had no control. From her body to her news, everyone seemed one step in front of her. First Ash. Then her family. Now all of Stonewall Crossing? For the first time in her life, she seriously considered hiding. If she didn't have the Gingerbread Festival, Christmas parades and every other holiday event to direct—she'd head for her cousin's place in West Texas. Peace, quiet and solitude.

"You two okay?" Hunter asked, a hand on both her and Fisher's shoulders, ever the big brother. "I haven't made you guys hug it out in years, but I will if I need to."

Fisher shook his head. "Nope. All good." He spun on his heel and went back into the kitchen.

That hurt. Until now, Fisher had been her go-to sibling. But, until now, she'd never kept secrets from him, and he was hurt.

"He's not happy," Ryder muttered.

"He'll get over it." Hunter sighed. "He's not one to hold a grudge."

"Let's hope not. Talk about awkward family dinners." Ryder laughed.

"You go on." She managed a smile. "I need a minute." She made it to the bathroom before she burst into tears, but it was close.

Ash did his best to smooth the single thick lock of black hair that crowned the top of his son's head. No luck. It bounced back, curling up like a curlicue antenna. Having his boy back with him was sheer heaven. "Seems to get bigger every day." He offered Curtis another block to stack.

Curtis smiled, leaning forward to grab his hands. "Daddy kiss."

Ash nodded, pulling his son close. "Missed you, too." He kissed his cheek.

Curtis nodded back, clapping his hands.

"He's missed you," his mother said, folding clothes

and packing them away in the chest of drawers. "Any luck finding a house? He'll need room before you know it."

"Nothing so far." He stacked one of the soft blocks on Curtis's head, and the boy shrieked with laughter when the block fell off.

"I'm guessing we walked into the hornet's nest?" Betty asked, peering at him through the bifocal lenses she kept on a chain around her neck. "I thought I was going to have to rescue Curtis before they jumped on you."

"I thought you were proposing?" his mother asked, continuing to unpack as if their conversation was nothing out of the ordinary.

"I did." He sighed, placing the block on Curtis's head again. No matter how bad his day was, his son's giggle was as bright as the Texas sun.

They both turned then, regarding him curiously.

"Turned me down before I could get down on one knee and ask properly." He shrugged.

"She's lovely," his mother pointed out. "All tall and willowy."

Shanna had been petite, with dark hair and light brown eyes—the exact opposite of Renata.

"She's beautiful." There was no point denying it. "Beautiful. Funny." He shook his head. "And stubborn. Too damn stubborn."

"Language," Betty chimed. "What reason did she give you?"

"Something about settling versus marrying for love and how she's capable of doing this on her own." He swallowed. "Like I said, stubborn."

The mothers were staring at him then.

"Do you?" his mother asked.

"Do I what?" he asked. "Love her? How can I love someone I don't even know?"

Betty clucked her tongue. "Well, dear, you knew her well enough to hop into bed and—"

"I get it." He held his hands up. They'd hopped, eagerly, and enjoyed every minute of that long, cold night wrapped up in each other.

"Maybe in time?" Betty offered. "Not everyone gets struck with a lightning bolt, after all."

Lightning bolts weren't their problem. Those they had in spades. "Maybe." He didn't hold out much hope. He wasn't sure his heart would ever heal enough to let someone else in. Or if he'd be brave enough to try again. Losing Shanna… It had almost destroyed him.

And Renata? It was only a matter of time before some man came along and fell head over heels for her. She'd get exactly what she wanted. Hell, what she deserved. So why did it rub him the wrong way to think about it?

Because his child's welfare would be affected, that's why.

"She said you were co-parenting." Betty tapped her chin again. "What does that mean?"

"It means they take turns, I think." His mother glanced his way. "Doesn't it? Sharing big decisions, that sort of thing?"

"You got me." He had no idea. She'd been acting like it was common knowledge. It wasn't. Raising Curtis on his own hadn't been a choice. And now, when he had the choice, he wouldn't choose to go it alone again.

"That's bad?" Betty asked.

"It's not good." He watched Curtis toddle across the room to his bag. He reached in, pulled out a few board books and carried them back to his blanket. "It's not what's best."

"Marrying her is best?" His mother pushed the drawer shut.

"Of course it is." He frowned at her, stacking up Curtis's soft blocks into a tower. "What's wrong with wanting to give my children a real family? To be there, day in and day out, through fevers and losing teeth and skinned knees and potty training?" Curtis was watching him, so he did the best he could to calm down. "All good, little man."

Curtis smiled and knocked the blocks wide.

"I wish life were that simple for me, Curtis," he said, running a hand over Curtis's silky-soft curls.

"Her father is a real charmer." His mother smiled. "His sons might want to beat the daylights out of you, but that Teddy Boone knows what it means to be a gentleman."

"And those eyes," Betty joined in. "Blue for miles."

"And married. Just in case you were wondering." He chuckled.

"I was just enjoying the view." His mother winked.

"Well, shucks." Betty sighed. "And rich to boot. I looked up the family on Google. Cattle. Oil. Land. Big-time. Renata is the only daughter."

Rich or not, the Boones were good people. "You'd never know it."

"I can't tell you what to do," his mother started. "And if I did, you'd just dig in and do the opposite anyway. But it seems to me you have a problem."

He sat back against the side of the bed. "I'm all ears, Mom."

"When you were little, and you had a rough day, what would I tell you?" she asked. "When you'd get disqualified in junior rodeo or get knocked down on the football field or have a girl break your heart?"

Betty sat in the rocking chair, glancing back and forth between them.

"I don't think that applies." He sighed, taking a block from his son and stacking them high again. "Now that I'm not a teenager."

"You just told Curtis you wished things were easier." She shrugged.

"I'm dying here." Betty slapped her hands on her knees. "You can't stop now."

His mother picked up her toiletry bag and carried it to the bathroom, pausing in the doorway. "Anything worth doing or having won't come easy."

He waited for her to disappear into the bathroom before making a face at Curtis. "Your gramma thinks she's imparting words of wisdom, Curt."

"I think they were very wise words indeed." Betty sat back in the rocking chair. "Better than any fortune cookie I ever got."

Ash laughed. He couldn't help it. And it felt good. He'd been wound too tight. The only thing that could have made it better? Having Renata here with them. If anyone needed a laugh, she did. But remembering the husky timbre of her laugh—and the effect it had on him—was dangerous.

"Daddy here." Curtis held out his block and sat in Ash's lap. "Go."

"You got it." He stacked the blocks up.

Curtis nodded, leaning back against his chest with a sigh.

Ash stacked them all, then wrapped his arms around his small son, drawing in his clean scent. Being away from Curtis for a few days had been hard. How was he supposed to co-parent with Renata? If he ever figured out what the hell co-parenting meant?

He sighed, tickling Curtis until his son was shrieking with laughter. He tugged up his shirt and blew raspberries on his little stomach, loving the free and easy glee his son expressed.

"Stop, Daddy." Curtis arched up, his arms stretching over his little head. "Stop." He kept giggling, pulling up his shirt and exposing more of his tummy.

"Stop?" Ash asked, still tickling.

Curtis shook his head. "No, Daddy. No stop."

Ash laughed, renewing his tickle attack and sending Curtis off on another giggle fit. There wasn't much he could do to fix the mess he and Renata had gotten themselves into. Might as well lose himself for a while in the simple joy of his son's laughter.

Chapter 8

Somehow the crying had turned to throwing up. Lots and lots of throwing up. But now that her stomach was empty, she was feeling almost human. Until she heard the knocking on her door. Rather insistent knocking.

"Coming," she said, not moving from her place on the bathroom floor. *Never mind.* She was too weak to move. "Come in," she called out with as much energy as she could muster.

"Renata? It's Kylee."

No, no, no, no...

"Are you in there?"

Hanging out in the bathroom.

"Renata." Kylee sounded worried.

By now they'd all know, of course. She'd officially bowed out of the family dinner—her stomach had demanded it. Kylee was here because she cared. Even if all Renata wanted at the moment was to be left alone. At least it wasn't her brothers. She'd had more than enough of them.

"We could hear you. And we're coming in," Kylee said, cracking the bathroom door.

We? An audience for her humiliation.

"Oh, Renata. Are you okay?" Kylee's sympathy was genuine.

The minute she saw Kylee try to kneel, Renata spoke up. "Don't you even think about getting down here. Then we'll both be stuck on the floor."

Kylee smiled, then stepped back.

Josie, Annabeth and Eden waited—wearing various expressions of concern.

She covered her face with her hands and groaned.

"Renata." Josie laughed. "It's okay."

"We've all been there," Annabeth added. "Literally, on the floor, throwing our guts up."

"Some of us multiple times." Eden laughed.

"We're here to offer moral support," Kylee finished.

"My brothers couldn't wait to spill the beans, could they?" She spoke through her hands.

"They're worried." It sounded like Annabeth. "So worried, they volunteered to watch all the kids. With Clara and Dad, of course. You've got a whole tribe of women on your side. What can we do?"

She had no idea what she was supposed to do. "I don't know," she murmured through her hands.

"First, drink this." Josie knelt on the floor at her side. "Peppermint tea. Always soothed my stomach."

It did smell delicious. And Christmassy, too.

"Having a hard time keeping things down?" Annabeth asked.

She uncovered her face, the smell of the tea too tempting to resist. Just holding the mug and breathing in the fresh mint offered relief. "It's going to get easier, right?"

The four of them smiled back.

"No?" She sighed.

"Up to moving this conversation out of your bathroom?" Annabeth asked.

Renata nodded, handing off her tea and pushing off the floor. Her stomach grumbled loudly. *I'm trying, baby. I promise. We'll sneak into the kitchen later.*

"The joys of pregnancy," Annabeth said.

"So far, not so joyful." Renata sat on her couch, pressing back into her seat.

"It *will* get easier," Josie said, nodding, as she perched on the arm of the chair where Kylee sat. "We're here to help."

"Does this offer of help extend beyond the pregnancy?" she asked. "Because I need help. As far as the baby goes… I'll worry about that tomorrow."

"Why tomorrow?" Eden asked.

"Well, I have a doctor's appointment—so I'll get a due date. D-Day right? I can start a countdown?"

"If baby cooperates." Josie smiled. "Babies have their own schedule. Starting now." She pointed at Renata's stomach.

All eyes focused on her stomach, including her own.

"Are they upset?" she asked, knowing the women

wouldn't need any clarification. She'd grown up wanting to make her brothers and father happy, especially after their mother died. It had been her goal, something she'd been aware of every day. Her mother had had the sort of smile that made everything better—Renata had done her best to fill the void she left. And now? It was hard to accept she was the reason they were all unhappy.

"They just want you to be happy, Renata." Annabeth used her perky voice.

"But they're not going to hurt Ash, right?" she asked. "Because they looked like they really wanted to."

No one said anything.

"Seriously?" she asked, her head falling back on the couch. "Poor Ash. I was the one waiting for him on the back porch. I was the one that suggested we spend the night together."

Josie giggled. "I knew it."

She giggled. "You did?"

"You're not exactly a shrinking violet, Renata." Kylee laughed.

"Should I be offended?" she asked, staring around at her sisters-in-law.

"I'm pretty sure it was a compliment." Eden laughed. "It was, right?"

Kylee nodded. "It was."

"You don't think there's the potential for something more? With Ash, I mean?" Annabeth asked. "He seems like a decent enough guy. And I caught a glance at his kid and he is adorable. So, there's an upside."

Renata was laughing now. "I'll make sure to list cute kid and decent guy in the pro column—if there's ever a need to make a list." But Annabeth had a point. "His son is precious, isn't he?"

And Ash was more than a decent guy. Not that any of them would ever know it. She couldn't let on about his misguided marriage proposal, not without dire consequences. Still, it was with the best intentions—he thought it was best for the baby. And that was what their relationship would be about: the baby. Nothing else. No matter how off the charts their attraction might be.

Ash paced the doctor's office. He had a list of questions a mile long, his stomach was in knots and the room was a good twenty degrees past bearable. He smiled at Renata again, tugged at his shirt collar and studied the obstetrics poster on the exam room wall. The miracle of birth. A time of excitement and anticipation—a new life, a fresh start.

He didn't feel any of those things. Pregnancy, to him, meant the beginning of the end. It meant sickness and frailty. Risk after risk. Uncertainty, pain and loss. Watching Shanna suffer, he'd vowed never to have another child. Now, here he was, preparing for fatherhood less than three years after that nightmare ordeal had begun.

There were so many questions without answers. But one stood out against all the rest. It was gnawing at his insides, making it impossible to focus on anything else. Was Renata healthy? And the baby? They were both fine? Once he knew that, he'd be able to relax. But he had to know that first.

"Ash?"

He turned. "What?"

"You okay?" She sat in a gown, looking just as uncomfortable as he felt. Only she was asking if he was okay.

Way to be supportive. "Fine. Sorry. Just reading…" He pointed at the poster he'd been blindly staring at.

She nodded, but he could tell she didn't believe him. "You didn't have to come today."

He glanced at her then. She wasn't thrilled that he'd been adamant about coming with her but, for him, it was necessary. He'd been up with nightmares most of the night—every worst-case scenario running through his mind. Renata wasn't Shanna. The only way to ease his fears and stop the comparisons was to hear it, himself, from her doctor.

Dr. Farriday arrived minutes later. She took one look at Ash and pointed at the stool in the corner. "Dr. Carmichael. Sit there for me." She was all smiles for Renata. "Congratulations, Renata. I was surprised to see your name on my patient schedule today."

"We're all surprised." Renata was smiling, teasing even.

While Ash was trying not to hyperventilate.

"Well, the bloodwork looks good so far. Numbers are where they need to be." Dr. Farriday was skimming over her chart. "In case you were wondering, you are pregnant."

Renata's laugh was surprised.

Ash couldn't. A thousand pounds of pressure seemed to be resting on his chest, threatening to crush him at any second. "How's everything else?" he asked. "She's healthy?" He was up, at her side, taking her hand in his. "No concerns. No need for more tests or scans? What, exactly, did her bloodwork show?"

"Am I missing something? Renata?" Dr. Farriday shook her head. "Is there a reason I should be concerned?"

Renata was looking at him—he could feel it. "No."

"Good. I'm not. Her bloodwork is perfect. There's no reason to worry." Dr. Farriday smiled. "She's young and strong, Dr. Carmichael. You make sure she gets plenty of rest and she's eating whatever she can keep down and this will be over before you know it." She winked at Renata. "And then the real fun begins."

Renata was squeezing Ash's hand. *She* was offering *him* support—the exact opposite of what she needed.

"You take care of her, she'll take care of the baby." Dr. Farriday was looking at him, waiting. "Believe me, you have the easier job."

In other words, *pull it together*. She was fine. She was healthy. And she needed him. Breathing was easier. "I can do that," he said, nodding.

Ash watched as Dr. Farriday lay Renata back, put a healthy dollop of gel on her stomach and pulled out a high-power stethoscope. "We're listening for heartbeats. You'll hear two. Mom, yours will be slower. The faster one is the baby."

Renata's grip tightened and her eyes locked with his. They shone with pure excitement. And it was contagious. When the rapid thump-thump filled the room, Ash's heart rate picked up, too.

"That's it?" she whispered, covering her smile with her hand. "That's the baby."

Their baby's heartbeat was strong and steady.

"Perfect," Dr. Farriday confirmed.

Renata laughed softly, so damn beautiful his chest hurt. He wiped away the tears that slipped from the corners of her eyes.

"Huh." Dr. Farriday moved the stethoscope, pressing a little harder. "Hold on. Well, it seems the Boone tradition continues." Dr. Farriday chuckled. "That, right there, is a third heartbeat."

"Two?" Renata whispered, her grip all but crushing his.

Two. He swallowed. Twins. They were going to have twins. And, terrified or not, she needed him. He smiled down at her, smoothing the hair from her forehead. "Go big or go home, right?" He winked.

"I like your way of thinking, Dr. Carmichael." Dr. Farriday pulled an ultrasound cart around, flipped on the monitor. The heartbeats disappeared, leaving the room oddly quiet. "Let's see what we can see."

But Ash focused on Renata. Twins. Did that increase her risk? More questions started forming. Questions that could wait, for the time being. He pulled a chair to her side and sat, doing his best to enjoy the moment—to savor this time. It would be easier if he could forget how terribly wrong Shanna's first prenatal appointment had gone.

"Looks good." Dr. Farriday was pointing at the

screen. "There's baby one." She clicked on the keyboard. "And there's baby two." More clicks. "I'll take a few pictures for you. And I'll make a disc for you to take home, too." She sat back, wiping the gel from Renata's stomach. "Questions?"

"Twins?" Ash asked. "What sort of risks are there?"

Dr. Farriday nodded. "No more than any other pregnancy, really."

"Delivery? Pre-term? Higher mortality rates?" He swallowed.

Dr. Farriday studied Ash. "You're worried about her. That's normal. But Renata is going to come through this. And the babies. Well, twins come early, but that's expected. I'll keep a close eye on her. If we're lucky, she'll go into labor on her own and deliver without any complications. If there are any complications, we'll be ready." She leaned forward. "But that's a ways down the road yet. She's healthy. The babies are healthy. Questions are good but worrying her isn't. Try to relax."

Good advice. If only he could listen to it.

"She's going to need you to take care of her. Little things like reminding her to get plenty of sleep, to eat a balanced diet, get some exercise—but not overdo it. It helps."

"I'll do my best, but that's easier said than done." He couldn't stop smiling when he saw her scowling at him. "I'm learning Renata Boone is all kinds of stubborn." And she was his. Healthy and alive and carrying his two babies. He was going to do whatever it took to keep them that way—all three of them.

"Another Boone trait?" Dr. Farriday laughed, handing him the ultrasound pictures. "Congratulations on the babies—I'm sure the wedding will be a big to-do. Waiting until after the holidays?"

"No wedding," Renata said, shrugging.

Dr. Farriday paused at the door, glancing back and forth between the two of them. "Oh? Well. All right."

It was on the tip of the tongue to mention that was all Renata's decision, but one glance at her red cheeks kept him quiet.

"No." Renata's cheeks turned a bright red as she carefully avoided his eyes. "Guess I should change. Give me a minute?"

Ash stood in the lobby, staring at the pictures, until Renata nudged him.

"Ready?" she asked, not waiting for his answer.

It had been a long time since hope and anticipation had surged through his blood, but now, because of these babies—because of Renata—it was there. While she was making their next few appointments, he watched her. The way she used her hands when she talked. Or wrinkled up her nose. Or how expressive her face was. Right now, she was all but vibrating with happiness. And when she flashed those blue eyes his way, he felt it, too. He glanced at the pictures of their babies. Babies. Twins. He tucked the pictures carefully into his wallet, a newfound sense of euphoria kicking in.

Today had gone from bad to incredible. There were no words to describe what he was feeling. But he didn't need words. What he needed was right beside him, talking and laughing and delighted about the babies growing in her belly.

His babies.

Life was going to be different now. But, dammit, it would be good. Her smile, her energy, woke him up in a way that excited him. And scared the crap out of him. Scared or not, he knew what he had to do. First up, talk to Teddy Boone.

Chapter 9

Renata hid behind one of the tall, elegantly potted Christmas trees placed strategically throughout the main tent. Hosting the ball at the refuge, located a stone's toss from the Lodge, allowed attendees an up-close-and-personal experience with the facility and the incredible work Archer did. But there were few places to escape from the heat, the noise and the countless clashing perfumes of a hundred or so women inside the tent. To say Archer's first charity ball was a success was an understatement. Archer, poor guy, was doing his best to be gracious, but it was taking a toll on him. Thank goodness his sweet wife, Eden, stayed by his side—her smiling, eloquent self—because her brother's patience was wearing thin.

At around the two-hour mark, Renata started to

relax. But once the excited butterflies wore off, good old-fashioned pregnancy-induced nausea set in. She'd downed water and eaten a few crackers from the appetizer trays—fresh air was her last hope.

Now that the success of the ball was a foregone conclusion, an early departure might be her only option. Tonight's focus should remain on the refuge and all the good work Archer did here—without any whiff of the scandal of her pregnancy tainting it. But navigating the crowd of perfume and cologne that stood between her and the exit without throwing up would be no small accomplishment. The other option, climbing over several corral fences—in an evening gown—would likely lead to the one thing she wanted to avoid: attention.

"Renata?" Josie appeared, offering her a glass of water. "Here." Kylee, Annabeth and Clara were behind her, wearing equally sympathetic expressions.

"You're looking a little pale." Annabeth smiled. "Doing okay?"

"I'm fine." It wasn't exactly a lie. According to the pregnancy ebook she'd downloaded, nausea was perfectly normal. So was being emotional. And tired. "But, don't judge me here, I'm wondering how hard Archer would take it if I snuck out."

"Archer would be fine." Kylee smiled. "But people will notice you leaving."

"They will?" She sipped her water. It was cool and clean and delightfully refreshing.

"You look amazing, Renata." Josie pointed.

"The lack of boots and jeans has been noted," Annabeth agreed.

Renata pressed her hand against her neck. "I *feel* horrible."

"Sorry, sweetie." Kylee patted her arm, giving her a full once-over. "But sneaking out might be a challenge."

She groaned. "I will never wear a dress again."

"Sit." Clara moved one of the folding chairs outside the tent. "Drink more water first. It might help."

"We'll keep you company until you feel better," Annabeth offered.

"I'm good. Some fresh air will perk me up. Go dance with your husbands." She appreciated the show of support, but she was fine being alone.

"To be honest, dancing is the last thing on my mind." Kylee sat in a chair just inside the large white tent, within range of a radiant space heater. "My ankles are swelling. I look like a bowling ball with legs. In a fancy dress."

"Well, my brother can't take his eyes off you," Renata assured her.

It was true. The twinge of jealousy was there, reminding her she had no man to look at her the way her brothers looked at their wives.

But I have you. She almost stroked her stomach. Almost. *Where's your father?* Her gaze swept the tent again. She'd assumed he'd be here. Since the doctor appointment, he'd made a habit out of popping up when she least expected it. His excuse? Questions about the gingerbread contest, interest in serving on a committee for some creek restoration project—even helping Irma find the burned-out bulb on the office Christmas tree.

He was there. Smiling. Acting like there was nothing out of the ordinary about him being there.

So where was he now? He could show up here without fabricating a reason. Things like big social events, especially ones connected to his co-workers, were logical functions for a new resident to attend. But there was no sign of him.

"Who are you looking for?" Annabeth asked.

Caught in the act.

"Ash Carmichael." Kylee ran her hands over her stomach.

Renata stared at her sister-in-law. "No—" She was a terrible liar.

"Please." Kylee shook her head. "I've known you for years now, Renata. I have never seen you…like that. It wasn't just nerves, either. You like him. Like him, like him." She smiled. "And he likes you. I don't know how Fisher missed it. An instant spark."

Fine. Yes. There was a *spark* between them. Who was she kidding? More like a full-blown, all-consuming blaze. That was all. Some bizarre physical connection that would, surely, fizzle out over time. Letting her imagination run wild or entertaining thoughts of things like love was ridiculous. She barely knew him. And she was pregnant—meaning not thinking straight. Allowing herself to possibly, maybe, fall for Ash Carmichael was out of the question. Except there was the very real possibility it was too late.

Way too late.

Stupid. Stupid. Stupid. Renata hugged herself and swallowed. Hard.

"More water?" Clara asked.

She shook her head. She wanted to go home. If her stomach would cooperate long enough, she'd make her getaway—over the fence if necessary.

"You're still green," Clara argued, taking her empty glass and heading for a refill.

Once it was clear she wasn't talking, conversation turned to the new playground equipment her father was funding for one of the city parks in honor of his grandchildren. It was important to him, a testament to how much he loved his grandchildren. Nothing was more important to her father than family.

Like Ash.

Her gaze wandered to the entrance again. And this time...

He was here.

Of course he was.

Instead of irritation or frustration, she felt... *Stop with the feelings.*

But looking at him, all manly and beautiful, had everything fading into the background. He was too damn beautiful. Crazy as it was, and it was, the tingles and warning bells and flutters returned. With a vengeance.

I am not falling for him. She swallowed. *Nope.*

He was talking to Quinton Sheehan and his cronies, laughing and smiling. Making her heart happy.

Being happy to see him was okay. It didn't mean anything. Stonewall Crossing was his home now, too, so they'd see each other. And there was the whole baby thing.

Still, should she feel *this* happy? Like, giddy?

Nope. Stop looking at him. Now.

But Clara was joining his group, sidling up beside him—whispering in his ear? All the nausea and clamminess and general ick quadrupled. Whatever Clara said had Ash's gray gaze searching the crowd. For her—she knew it.

Dammit.

The moment Ash's eyes found her, Renata was done for.

He was walking her way, dangerously handsome in his tuxedo, a crooked grin on his face. The closer he got, the harder it was to breathe. The look on his face, heat simmering in his gaze, was impossible to ignore. Or misread.

I can think of worse things than being overwhelmingly attracted to the mother of my child. His words replayed, over and over.

It was hot. Very hot. And her stomach was in the midst of a series of spins and dives that made it impossible to stay seated. Not if the women were going to keep teasing. And he was closing in on her. Besides, if she continued to sit here, he'd join them. There was no way she'd be able to hide what she was feeling. They'd take one look at her and know it.

She was up and moving toward him before she had time to think things through. And once she was inches away from him, her senses were flooded with things like his scent and his warmth and…him. "Ash." Apparently, that was all she could muster.

"Renata." His voice was gruff and low.

Try again. "You…look nice in a tux."

"Thank you." He swallowed. "You look hot."

His serious expression had her laughing.

She liked it when he was looking at her mouth like that. Like he wanted to kiss her. The way he was looking at her right now. It would be better if they weren't surrounded by Stonewall Crossing's finest.

"Clara said you were feeling poorly again?"

"Your fault." She shrugged.

His eyes widened and his knock-the-air-from-her-lungs grin spread. "Guilty." He didn't sound the least bit bad about it. He looked a little too...pleased with himself, actually. "Up for a dance?" He held his hand out.

Bad idea. "Are my feet in any danger?" His hand was warm around hers.

"I promise to make it up to you later." The matter-of-fact delivery almost kept her bones from melting. Almost.

"Ash," she whispered, willing her body to behave—with no success. Glancing around them confirmed her fears. People were staring. Smiling, but staring. And talking. People like Winnie Santos and Lola Stephens. Her stomach dropped.

Say no. Dancing with him? A colossal mistake. But *No, thank you* or *Have a nice evening* or *Good night* wouldn't come out and, somehow, they ended up on the dance floor.

"Stop looking at me like *that*." She pleaded, far too aware of the man holding her close.

"Like what?" He frowned. "You just have a dirty mind, Miss Boone."

Her mouth dropped open and she was laughing again.

"You're beautiful, Renata." It was a whisper. His hand rested at the base of her spine. Big. Strong. Warm. "And sexy as hell."

He was playing with her. And loving every minute of it. The problem was—so was she.

Ash was sweating. Nervous.

He could do this. He liked having Renata in his arms. He liked how easy the banter was between them. And the gleam in her eyes when she looked at him? He definitely liked that. All it took was one look, and anticipation was pumping through his veins—for this woman.

This could work. This, they, could be good. But she had to give them a chance.

Teddy's reluctant blessing—and warning—still rang in his ears.

My daughter deserves a man's love and loyalty. Anything less is intolerable. He'd cleared his throat, his blue eyes sharp. *You understand me, son?*

Yes, sir. He'd forced the words out, feeling like a fraud.

Having this... It will mean... She'll know you have my blessing. This was her mother's. It's special. Teddy's voice had wavered as he's handed over the filigree ruby ring. *Like my daughter.*

Now Ash stood, holding her close, the ring burning a hole through his pocket, trying to muster the courage to ask—plead if need be—to give their babies the family they deserved.

"I found a place I like today. The old Gruber place?"

Her blue eyes widened. "I used to call it the fairy-tale house."

Ash knew that, courtesy of Teddy. The Grubers used to host parties throughout the years and, according to her father, Renata had looked forward to them most. She'd been entranced by the house's dramatic steepled rooftops, gabled windows, stained glass and carved wooden doors—all imported by Charles Gruber's relative sometime back in the early eighteen hundreds.

"I was sad when I heard the family was selling it." She paused, frowning. "It's a lot of house for you, isn't it?"

He shook his head. "Big enough for half a dozen kids, me, the wife and the mothers. We'll put the mothers in the carriage house, of course." He ignored her shock and kept right on talking. "It's mostly renovated. The kids will be spoiled, getting their own bathrooms. The living room and dining room are large, built for a big family." He waited.

She blinked. "A half a dozen kids?"

He couldn't help but smile. "I want a big family. The wife can decide, since she's the one who has to carry them for nine months."

She blinked again, stiffening in his arms. "I'm sure she will appreciate that. Very considerate."

"I'll always do my best to be considerate of your thoughts and feelings." He meant it.

She froze, in the middle of the dance floor, her blue eyes wide.

It had been a long time since he'd felt anything but pain in his chest, but now he felt something else. Panic, maybe. A little fear. And something else. A tug. In his chest. Deep down. He cared about Renata—making this far easier than he'd expected. "Renata Boone, I need to ask you something."

She shook her head, her eyes wide. "No, you don't, Ash. Not here."

"Yes, here. In front of your family." He leaned closer. "And four brothers that might very well string me up if this goes wrong."

She shook her head. "Ash, please—"

He stepped back, putting enough space between them to end her plea. There was no going back now. He pulled the ring from his pocket and held it out, the red stone sparkling under the hundreds of lights strung overhead—

It happened so quickly he didn't have time to react. One minute she was shaking her head, wide eyes fixed on the ring, the next she was throwing up all over the dance floor and his polished shoes.

The whole tent seemed to erupt.

"Oh God," Renata groaned, covering her face with her hands.

He was too startled to do much more than pull her close. "Are you okay?"

"No," she whispered. "No, I'm not okay. I can't believe you... Why did you do this?" She pushed away from him and straightened, attempting to hide how shaken and upset she really was.

"Oh, Renata, honey." Clara was there, leading the Boone women onto the dance floor for a group rescue.

All he could do was stand there while they took her away, feeling like an ass. He'd expected shock. Possibly resistance. But there had been betrayal on her face—and humiliation.

Teddy Boone was doing his best not to laugh as he crossed the dance floor, offering Ash a handkerchief. "I'm pretty sure that's not how you imagined it." He chuckled then.

"No, sir," he agreed, waving off the offer of his handkerchief as he surveyed his shoes. "I should check on her."

"Let Clara take care of her." Teddy sighed, his gaze sweeping the tent. "I'm afraid Renata's…reaction will require some damage control."

Ash frowned, assessing the room.

Winnie Santos was smiling, animatedly talking to a group of women—Lola Stephens among them.

"Dammit," he ground out. "She's not going to be happy."

"No, son, she's not." Teddy sighed. "But you can make it a little easier."

"Tell me how."

"Stonewall Crossing's a small town, Ash. And Renata is well loved." He nodded at his sons. "You need to win them over, and they'll stop at nothing to help you win my daughter's affection."

It was his turn to feel nauseous. "Isn't that a little manipulative? I don't want to force her into—"

"Oh, you won't. We both know how stubborn that girl is when she makes up her mind." The older man clapped him on the shoulder. "But they won't run you out of town if they know you *want* to marry her—even if she does say no." His brows rose.

"Oh." He nodded. There was no arguing with the older man's wisdom. Stonewall Crossing was his home now, but what happened next could determine whether or not he remained welcome here.

"She okay?" Hunter asked, eyeing Ash with suspicion.

"Ash might have gotten her a little riled up." Teddy smiled. "She'll be fine."

Hunter shot his father a sidelong look. "What's going on?"

Teddy looked at him, shrugging. "Up to you."

Ash pulled the ring from his pocket—right about the time Fisher arrived.

"What the hell?" Fisher practically growled. "I don't know what you said to her but—" He broke off, his gaze falling to the ring Ash held.

Hunter chuckled. "That was her answer?"

"I was still asking the question when, well, you saw." He looked down at his feet.

"Sounds like an answer to me," Fisher bit out, turning his scowl on his father. "You're telling me you're okay with this?"

Teddy Boone's brows rose and his jaw locked. "I am. And so should you be. That baby is his."

"Babies," Ash interjected.

"Of course." Teddy chuckled.

"She doesn't love him." Fisher's posture eased, the respect he bore for his father obvious. But the edge to his voice remained. "He doesn't love her."

"I'm not so sure about that." Teddy spoke with such confidence even Ash almost believed.

"Is Renata okay?" When Lola Stephens joined them, he wasn't sure. But she was craning her neck to peer around Fisher Boone. Her gaze darted between them before honing in on the ring and instantly brightening. "Oh my! I knew it. I knew it. Ask Carl. I just knew you were sweet on our girl."

Ash didn't argue.

"And that, right there, is enough to make any girl a little overexcited. Winnie's over there trying to turn it into something it's not—you know how that woman is." She shook her head.

"Well," Teddy interrupted. "Sometimes there's a grain of truth to things."

Lola perked up.

"We might have gotten things a little out of order." Ash mustered as much enthusiasm as possible. "But I have every intention of remedying things as soon as I can."

Lola was all smiles. "Sometimes things can get a little carried away."

Fisher's jaw looked ready to pop off.

"I'm glad to hear it'll all work out in the end." Lola hooked her arm through Teddy's, excited. "And that there are still folk that believe in old-fashioned values."

It took no time for word to spread. He smiled, shook hands and got so many congratulations it felt like the town had accepted they were already engaged. But he knew the truth. And tomorrow, when he faced her, he suspected she wouldn't share in the enthusiasm. Or be eager to accept his proposal.

Chapter 10

Renata pulled on her mittens, zipped up her down coat and tugged her brightly colored knit hat on. It was twenty-eight degrees, pitch black and she had a flat tire. She could call one of her brothers...and they'd come and drag her home.

Home.

She rested her forehead on the steering wheel.

She didn't run. Ever. But she'd never, ever been so humiliated. The whole town had been there, watching as Ash's obvious proposal went horribly, horribly wrong. She groaned. What choice did she have? Facing Stonewall Crossing now—her family—set her stomach to churning all over again. And there was absolutely nothing left in it.

But it wasn't just the spectacle of her absolute em-

barrassment. Betrayal and hurt battled for dominance.
Her father... He'd given Ash his blessing? She'd told
him, and her brothers, that they weren't getting married. But clearly her opinion didn't matter.

Of course her father wanted her to marry the father
of her child—that's what she wanted, too. If there was
love and commitment and all the things an engaged
couple should feel. She and Ash weren't that couple.
And, still, her own father wanted her to marry him?
After telling her and showing her, every day of his life,
the necessity of love to a marriage and family, how
could he believe she'd accept Ash's proposal?

What was worse... If she'd seen even a glimmer
of something, beyond fear and panic, in his eyes—
some hint of affection—she might have accepted his
proposal. Because...because of what she was feeling
for him.

She shook her head, firmly locking away that co-
nundrum for now. Not tonight.

Whether or not the proposal had happened, word
was out. And now Stonewall Crossing was abuzz over
her impending marriage to the handsome new veterinarian. And the pregnancy? The constant ping of congratulations texts and well wishes seemed to suggest
everyone was overjoyed at her pregnancy—due to her
imminent marriage.

That would all change when she rejected him. And
she would reject him.

"Just because you two are a wonderful mistake
doesn't mean marrying your father would turn out

that way," she said to her stomach and sighed. "Is it so wrong to want to be happy? To want love?"

The truck cab remained eerily quiet. She lifted her head and peered out into the dark night. Thick white flakes were falling, blanketing the land in frigid silence.

Sitting here in the cold wasn't an option. She knew how to change a tire. Her daddy believed in teaching all of his kids basic vehicle maintenance. Tires, oil, windshield wiper fluid, all that stuff. She was a confident, independent, capable woman, dammit. And, right now, the need to be self-sufficient was overwhelming.

"Let's do this, babies," she said out loud, trying to bolster her fragile spirits.

The minute she pushed the truck door open, she was blasted by the icy night air. Tugging her coat tighter around her, she slid from the cab and walked around to the truck bed. The beam of her flashlight cut a wide swath in the dark, her isolation more than a little unnerving. Not that she was going to regret her mad dash from the safety of her home. Or wish she'd simply retreated to the privacy of her apartment versus driving an hour into no-man's land in the middle of the night.

"So not helping." With the flashlight propped on the truck bed, she rifled through the toolbox until she had all the parts needed for the tire change. "See, all good."

Now came the fun part.

The tire was screwed under the truck bed. Which meant she'd have to lie down, unscrew the tire and roll it out. Then there was the whole pumping up the jack thing. Just leaning against the side of the truck had caused the fabric of her gown to go damp—and freezing.

"Sorry, guys," she mumbled. "I'll make this as quick as I can."

Not quick enough. Opening the rack that held the tire in place was harder than it looked. The frost, probably. Her thick mittens didn't help, snagging and catching on the screws and brackets, so she tugged them off and threw them aside. Within seconds, her fingers were so cold it was hard to keep a solid grip on the pliers she was using.

"Stupid," she ground out, both hands gripping the handles. "Stupid."

A vehicle's high beams hit her car, illuminating the underside of her truck and the tire bracket.

"Ha!" she cried, managing to twist the screw a full turn before her fingers went numb and the tool slipped from her hand. It fell, heavy, to the grass right by her head.

"That could have hurt," she ground out, her heart hammering in her ears. If it had hit her on the head, then what? She was in the middle of nowhere, hours from help. "I'm sorry," she whispered, running her hands over her stomach. "I'm so sorry." Her eyes stung, like her fingertips. But this time, the stinging had nothing to do with the temperature and everything to do with her predicament.

"What was I thinking?" Right now, the only person to blame was herself.

She hadn't realized the vehicle had pulled onto the shoulder of the road beside her until she noticed the ground beneath her was flooded with light. The roar of an engine, the slam of a door...the crunch of boots on the newly fallen sleet.

Followed by an all-too-familiar voice. "Please tell me you're not under there." The instant relief—and something far more alarming—Ash Carmichael's presence caused vanished. He was angry.

He was angry? *He* was the reason she was in this situation. Sort of. She stayed where she was, shivering and fuming.

"Renata," he snapped. "It's freezing."

"I know. Believe me, I know. If it wasn't, I'd already have the stupid spare out of the stupid rack and the stupid truck jacked up so I could change the stupid tire," she snapped right back. Now that she knew the babies could hear her, cussing felt wrong.

He crouched down. "Come out from under there."

She closed her eyes, knowing she should listen. The bolt was stuck, the tire was stuck—she was stuck.

"Dammit, Renata. I know you're mad at me, but it's too cold for you to do this now."

He was right. But—

"The cold isn't good for the babies. Please get up," he said, crouching and peering under the truck. Arm extended, he reached out to her.

How could she argue with that? She couldn't. And he knew it. But she wasn't about to take more help than was necessary. She slid out, carefully, leaning aside so as not to hit her head on the rear bumper. But once she was sitting up, the effects of the cold were harder to ignore. Try as she might, she couldn't pull herself up.

He held his hand out again. "Let me help."

She glared up at him before taking his hand, hating the instant warmth that his touch caused. It wasn't fair. Nothing about tonight was fair. *Except he's here and we're not stuck on the side of the road all night long in freezing temperatures.* Not that this moment of clarity stopped her from shoving her hands into her pockets and looking his way.

But he was shining a light on the flat. "Someone coming to help fix this?"

"I've got it."

She heard Ash's sigh.

"I can change a flat," she added.

He stared at her, his anger surprising her. "I'm sure you can, Renata. But whether you can or not, you *shouldn't* be. It's freezing. And late. And dark." He pulled her hands from her pockets and rubbed them between his. "Your hands are like ice cubes. Where are your gloves?"

"Where are yours?" She stared at their hands. Big hands. Rough hands. Warm. She had very fond memories of his hands. *Really?* She was going to go there now? But her attempt to pull her hands away failed as his hold tightened on hers.

"Renata." That tone. All soft and deep and spine tingling. Warning bells sounded.

"No, Ash." She yanked her hands from his. There would be no spine tingles tonight. "Leave me alone."

Another sigh. "That's not going to happen. I will take you home—"

"I'm not going home," she interrupted him, doing her best not to shiver.

He stared at her, his face too shadowed for her to clearly read what was going through his brain. Still, the hoarse "Please," tugged at something inside. "Tomorrow, when it's light, we'll get your tire changed and you can go to Fire Gorge."

"How did you know where I was going?" she asked.

"I didn't. I hoped. All I knew was you were gone. Your dad said something about Fire Gorge once—how it was your place to get away. I figured, after tonight, you'd want to get away. So I started driving, hoping."

There were so many things about what he said that weakened her resolve to stay mad.

His voice was soft. "I get that you're mad at me, but I'd like to apologize—"

"An apology?" Her throat was tight. She braced herself.

"Apologize. Grovel. Beg—right here, on my knees if you want." He shifted from one foot to the other.

"You think that's what I want?" Her voice shook. "What I want is to go back in time and fix...*this*." Before the ball and throwing up and seeing her mother's ring in his hand and the expectant smile on her father's face. The images collided, stoking her temper. "I want you to leave. That's what I want."

His entire body stiffened, an odd choking cough escaping him before he growled, "I'm not leaving you out here."

"I can't go home right now. I need...space. From

everyone." She hugged herself. "From my dad. The town. You."

"Fine." He cleared his throat. "I'll change the tire. But you have to sit in my truck until then, please." He was changing her tire so she could leave. Which was what she wanted. "Come on, Renata. This temperature can't be good for the babies," he pleaded.

He wasn't playing fair. But then again, she hadn't given him much of a choice. She was being irrationally stubborn here. "Okay." She forced the word out, shoved the tools into his hands and hurried to his truck.

It was hard to sit there. While she was soaking up the warmth of the heater, he was crawling under her truck, doing what she asked, in the freezing cold—so she could leave. While it was snowing. In the middle of the night.

Guilt kicked in.

The longer it took, the colder it became, the greater the guilt. She was toasty warm and he was still under her truck, trying to open the damn tire rack. According to the temperature reading on his dashboard, it was hovering around eighteen degrees.

His gloveless fingers were probably beyond numb by now.

"This is ridiculous," she mumbled. "Your mother isn't normally a horrible and selfish person. I'm sorry for losing my head, babies." She opened the truck window a crack. "Ash," she called out. "Come warm up."

It took him a few minutes, but he joined her. He sat, cheeks flushed and nose bright red, staring straight ahead. He flexed his equally red fingers and muttered, "It's stuck. The screw is stripped, I think."

Still, he'd kept trying. For her. Even though this wasn't his fault. Not really. Not the broken-down-on-the-side-of-the-road part anyway. She was the one who had thrown up all over him and caused a spectacle. She was the one who had run away. He'd been the one left to deal with the aftermath.

She studied his profile. Tension bracketed his mouth. The muscle in his jaw clenched tight. Still oh so handsome. And kind. He was a good man. If only… She swallowed. If only he felt *something* for her. Like the way she might, possibly—probably—feel about him. She covered her face with her hands, wanting to hide— needing a buffer between them and *all* the feelings.

"What do you want me to do?" he whispered.

She glanced his way, too tired to fight—or drive— anymore. "I just need to get my keys and my purse. If you'll still give me a ride?"

Those gray eyes met hers. The sadness was real. Deep. Raw. Pressing in on her until she had to look away. "I'll get them. Stay here." He was out of the truck before she could argue.

She wrapped her arms around her waist, her gaze following him as he jogged to her truck. Maybe— no, definitely—she'd overreacted by running tonight. Hopefully, tomorrow things wouldn't seem so over-whelming. After a good night's sleep, she'd wake up and she wouldn't be in love with the father of her babies and her heart wouldn't be at risk.

* * *

What I want is to go back in time and fix...this. Few words had ever hurt as much.

Shock or not, he wouldn't wish this pregnancy away.

Neither would she. What had happened tonight had upset her. Her reaction was undoubtedly compounded by the additional pregnancy hormones. And the Boone stubborn streak her father had reminded him of. Renata and these babies? He knew exactly how she felt about them. Her face had lit up at the doctor's office when they'd heard their babies' heartbeats. She wanted them—loved them. But not him.

Through the front windshield, he saw her, knees drawn up, hands over her face, looking fragile and small. And it was a kick to the gut. Unintentionally or not, he'd outed her secret in a very public way. But how could he have known the proposal would go so terribly wrong?

He owed it to her to fix this—somehow, some way. Did he have any ideas? Hell no. Considering his last idea had landed him covered in vomit and Renata running for the hills, he really needed to think this one through. For now, he was happy he'd convinced her to give up her midnight drive to a place that was fifty miles from nowhere. It was a start.

He pulled himself into the truck cab and slammed the truck door, sealing out the surprisingly bitter cold.

"Thank you." She took the purse he offered, still huddled in her seat.

He nodded, wanting to say something—anything—

to ease the tension between them. "I am sorry," he murmured.

In the deafening silence of the truck cab, there was no way she'd missed the apology. But sitting there, hoping she'd say something or—dream on—accept his apology wasn't going to make the drive into town go faster. He was bone tired as it was. If he was, she had to be. And the babies... Well, they all needed their beds. The sooner, the better.

He put the truck in gear and headed back home, the quiet crushing in on him and making him squirm. If she didn't want to listen to him apologize, he'd change gears entirely. Neutral ground was good. Curtis. Or the mothers. Or his work. Even the Gruber place she was so fond of. But a glance her way told him the conversation window was closed.

For a moment, it hurt to breathe.

She'd shifted in the seat, facing him. There was no sign of the stress or anger that had rolled off her when she'd been awake. Instead, she was young and calm... And more beautiful than ever. Something about this brave, stubborn woman had captured his attention.

He'd make this right between them. He had to.

The drive to the Lodge seemed to take twice as long as it should've. But when he'd finally parked, the sight of her sleeping peacefully made it impossible to wake her. He scooped her into his arms, comforted by her body's warmth. The brush of her breath on his throat set the hair on the back of his neck straight up. And the press of her hand against his chest knocked the rhythm of his heart. Her head lolled back against his shoulder, and he stared down at her face.

Affection rolled over him. Real affection. With a healthy dose of surprising territorialism. *Dammit.* But coming face-to-face with Fisher, pacing before the fireplace, demanded his overwhelming reaction to Renata would wait—for self-preservation's sake.

"Thank God," Fisher whispered, staring at his sister with unveiled concern. "Where was she?"

"On her way to Fire Gorge," he answered.

Fisher shook his head. "Are you kidding me? She's okay?"

He hoped so. He'd been an hour behind her—an hour she'd been stuck on the side of the road. "Should probably put her to bed before she wakes up."

"Too late," Renata murmured, those blue eyes going wide when she realized she was in his arms. She slipped free, her expression remote. "I'm good."

As soon as she was on her feet, Fisher was pulling her in for a hug. "You're too stubborn for your own good, you know that?"

"It runs in the family," she returned, melting into her twin without resistance. "Dad—"

"Doesn't know you took off." Fisher held her away, his expression stern. "I lied, told him you'd gone straight to bed. Good damn thing he didn't see your truck missing."

"He will tomorrow." Her eyes bounced to Ash. "My truck's got a flat. Ash tried to help but the bolt was frozen on." She broke off, yawning.

"We can worry about that tomorrow. You need

sleep." So did the babies. But Ash decided not to add that part.

"I'm going." Her big blue eyes met his. "I… Remember what I said, Ash, please."

Which part? That she was mad at him? That she wanted space? The fact that she'd said she'd go back in time and erase what had happened between them if she could? Erase that night? The babies? Everything? The lump in his throat prevented him from saying a word.

"I'll get someone to help me with the truck." Without another word or look, she disappeared down the main hallway.

He stood there watching her, the lump in his throat damn near choking him. She wanted space—needed space. But dammit, he didn't.

Fisher was studying him with open hostility. He should have expected the fist. The impact was hard and fast. His jaw felt like it had been slammed into a wall. If that wall was Fisher Boone's fist.

"Shit," Ash ground out, supporting his jaw and reeling from the impact.

"You might have my dad fooled, but I know you proposed because you knocked her up," Fisher said, anger edging every syllable.

Ash was too busy seeing stars to choose his words carefully. "I have a responsibility. But marrying her—"

This time, Fisher made impact with his stomach—knocking the air clean out of Ash's lungs.

"Damn. It," Ash hissed.

"My sister doesn't need your misguided pity proposal, you son of a bitch. She deserves a husband.

You've been married before so you should know good and well what I'm saying," he growled. "If you don't love her, you leave her the hell alone. I mean it. She's got plenty of people who do love her. We're ready and willing to take care of her and her kids."

"Now, hold on." Ash saw red then. It was still hard to breathe, let alone talk, but he forced himself to stand tall and stare Fisher in the eye. "But I do *want* to be with her. I want to be her husband, and I'm going to raise my children with her." He stood a little straighter, ignoring the pull in his side and the throb in his jaw. "You can beat the shit out of me, Fisher. It won't change how I feel."

Jaw locked, hands fisted, Fisher stared at him for a long time. But Ash wasn't about to back down. Physically, he didn't stand a chance against Fisher Boone. Hell, he'd be feeling the effects of Fisher's fists for days to come. But the only choice he had was to stand his ground. He moved his jaw side to side and winced.

"Be happy I was holding back." He sighed.

"That was holding back?" Ash murmured.

"Dammit, Ash… I like you." Fisher groaned. "But, she's my sister. She… When she finally falls, that'll be it. She'll be all in. Forever." Fisher's gaze sharpened. "If you can't do the same, I'm asking you—man-to-man—to walk away. Because if you bail or change your mind or meet someone else, she's not the sort to recover."

If Fisher was hoping to scare him off, it was having the opposite effect. The thought of having Renata at his side for the rest of his life filled him with a surprising peace. Whatever the future held, he wanted her in it.

He knew that. Accepted it. And held on—tight. "I'm not going anywhere—not unless she sends me away."

Fisher was staring at him again. Ash stared right back.

"I still have to get her to say yes."

Fisher smiled. "She'll make you work for it."

He nodded. "That's fine. I can be just as stubborn as she is."

"Oh, I seriously doubt that." Fisher clapped a hand on his shoulder. "You're going to need reinforcements. Free tomorrow?"

His nod was slow.

"Come to Archer's refuge tomorrow. Six o'clock."

"Now you're going to help me?"

"Not just me." Fisher's grin was hard. "Our brothers."

The Boone brothers? He'd seen the looks on their faces tonight—he knew none of them were sold on this. "Why?"

"My father gave you my mother's ring, which tells me how much he wants this marriage." His jaw clenched. "I just rattled your skull and cracked a rib and you're still standing. That can only mean one thing. You love my sister. And, dammit, I want my sister happy."

Fisher's words hung with him throughout the next day. Love wasn't part of this. It couldn't be, he wasn't equipped for that. His heart wasn't healed yet—neither was he. But, even after a day learning the fine points of the patient management system used by the veterinary hospital, Fisher's words remained. And when Ash headed to Boone Ranch and the horse refuge at precisely six o'clock, he wasn't sure how to feel or what to expect. He parked his truck in front of the business offices and followed the directions Eden gave him to the stables.

He walked past several horse stalls, appreciating the setup. Horses peered over their stall doors, ears swiveling and nostrils blowing—welcoming him. He paused, eyeing an especially fine brown buckskin with a white blaze on his nose. The horse seemed to be checking him out, too, bumping Ash's chest with his nose.

"Hello to you, too," he murmured.

"On the market for a horse?" A man asked, watching the horse with interest.

"Maybe." Hell yes, he wanted one. He missed having a horse, having a place of his own to ride out and explore. Now, well, he had the land and the house. About all he was missing was a horse. He'd need to check out the stables at Gruber House first. Make sure they were safe and sound. "Looking for Archer Boone."

The man nodded. "This way."

Ash followed him through the barn and beyond to a yard where saddled horses waited.

He braced himself. He knew how Fisher wasn't sold on the marriage, but the rest of them? Well, he was about to find out. He stood his ground. He didn't relish the idea of the other Boones taking shots at him, but he was hoping it wouldn't come to that.

Archer frowned. But he was always frowning.

Hunter was openly sizing him up. Not aggressive so much as assessing. He could respect that. They didn't know him well.

Ryder. Well, Ryder Boone looked ready to beat the

shit out of him. Eager, almost. If their roles had been reversed, he'd probably be in the same boat.

"Glad you came." Hunter broke the silence, his gaze zeroing in on the humdinger of a bruise Fisher had left on his jaw. "After last night, well—"

"You were going to propose?" Archer asked.

"I was." He cleared his throat. "I am."

Archer's gaze narrowed. "She doesn't want to marry you?"

He had to admire the man's straightforward attitude. "No." No point dragging this out.

Ryder chuckled. "Well, that was easy." He turned back to tightening the cinch on his saddle. "No one, and I mean no one, is going to get our sister to change her mind."

"Dad wants this." Fisher didn't bother pretending he felt the same.

"Dad's wrong." Ryder glared at Ash.

"This wouldn't be the first time you two didn't see eye to eye." Hunter smiled at his younger brother.

"He brought her home last night, carried her inside and—after he stood there and took that from me— he tells me he wants to marry her." Fisher spoke with grudging admiration. "I might have even cracked a rib or two."

Ash nodded. "Might."

All four of them faced him then. They loved their sister deeply. Up until now, it had been their job to protect her. But now?

"You *want* to marry her?" Hunter asked.

He cleared his throat. "Yes. Very much." Admitting the truth felt good.

The brothers exchanged a meaningful look. But he couldn't tell if it was a good look or a bad look.

"Dammit," Ryder bit out the curse. "We're going to need more beer for this."

"You have no idea what you're attempting." Archer crossed his arms over his chest. "Our sister is a force of nature."

Ash nodded. He knew. Oh, he knew. It was one of the things he liked best. Damn. Since he was telling the truth, maybe it was time to accept that his feelings for Renata were turning into something…more.

"Let's get to work," Hunter said, his jaw set with determination.

This would soon be his family—Curtis and the babies' family. Maybe, with her brothers' help, he'd stand a chance at convincing Renata how good it could be between them. To do that, there needed to be less space between them and more time spent together. Preferably alone.

Chapter 11

Renata took the last bite of her gingerbread cookie and sat back in her chair, staring into the dying embers of the fire. It was after midnight and she was sneaking milk and cookies like a little girl. She smiled, wrapping the embroidered blanket tighter around her legs and relaxing against the side of the high wingback leather chair.

It was nice to pretend, for a little while longer, that all the fuss and fervor that had become her life didn't exist. The Lodge library was her personal oasis. The book-lined room was deserted and quiet, both things she craved at the moment. The Christmas tree, all lit up and decorated, was an added bonus.

Her eyes had popped open to a new day—a day full of choices. Choosing to let a tow truck repair her truck.

Choosing to stay here versus escaping to Fire Gorge. Choosing to call in sick so she could delay the several dozen interrogations she'd have to suffer through when she went to work. And choosing to stay in her room no matter how hard her father or Clara tried to change her mind. It wouldn't last forever, she knew that. But she deserved twenty-four hours.

Once the nausea and vomiting stopped, life would be easier. She hoped. "Growing babies is hard work, guys." She'd played the digital recording of her babies' heartbeats several times through. The sound was oddly soothing. And the little blips on the screen? They were real. They were hers. They were pure goodness. And she was beyond excited to meet them. "Not too early though, okay?" She'd been reading her pregnancy book. When she wasn't freaking out over all the things that could go wrong, she was amazed at what was happening inside her body. No wonder she was so tired all the time.

"We have the parade and the Gingerbread Festival soon. It's our job to make sure everything goes off without a hitch, okay?" She looked down at her stomach. "Your momma knows her way around an event, don't you worry. And when it's all over, we'll slow down, take naps and relax."

"Renata?" Ash's voice startled her.

She pressed herself into the corner of the chair and froze. Ash was the last person she wanted to see. If she stayed super quiet, he'd go away. That was what she wanted, wasn't it?

The door slid open.

Dammit. She tensed, far too excited that he was here. What about the whole wanting space thing? Not that she actually *wanted* space. The door shut. Had he left? Disappointment welled.

The thump of boot heels crossing the wooden floor had her smiling. Widely. The sound was muffled now—because he was beside her, on the thick hand-braided carpet.

"You're still here." His voice was low. Deep. Enticing.

She bit her lip to fight her smile. But that didn't stop her heart from thumping.

"No Fire Gorge?" he asked.

She shook her head, worried her voice would give her away.

"I'm glad." It was almost a whisper.

She glanced at him. Even in the dim lighting, his smile managed to knock the air from her lungs. "You are?"

He stared down at her just long enough for her bones to begin to melt, then crossed to pull the leather settee in close and sit. "Talking to the babies?"

She blinked, nodding—willing her thoughts and her body to behave. She should tell him to leave, remind him of the whole space request thing… Why did he have to look like that? All manly and desirable and capable. Her dreams reminded her regularly of just how capable he was. In great detail.

His grin was a thing of beauty.

This needed to stop. Immediately. "Ash." She liked

saying his name. "Ash." Already said that. "I came in here to sit in the dark, for some peace and quiet."

"I can be quiet," he said, turning to face the fire and leaning back against the other arm of her chair. "And peaceful."

She wasn't feeling remotely peaceful at the moment. The exact opposite was more like it. Her stomach growled.

"Hungry?" He glanced over his shoulder.

She sucked in a deep breath to ease the flutter in her chest. "I've had three gingerbread cookies and a large glass of milk. I'm covered."

"That's not a meal." He was frowning now.

"I'll be happy if I can keep it down." She sighed, noting the deep blue tones the firelight brought out in his dark hair. If she wanted, she could run her fingers through the ebony silkiness. It would be easy. Natural, almost. She fisted her hand. She did not want to. Who was she kidding? She really, *really* did.

"I'm sorry this has been so hard on you. Eventually, that will stop. You'll have cravings and get round." He turned, resting his elbow on the seat cushion—next to her. He was too close, crowding in on her. And she liked it. "It's a good thing, considering." His tone was velvet.

"Considering the babies." The babies were his motivation. Not her.

"You feeling okay?" he asked.

It was an innocent enough question, but it reminded her of the doctor's appointment and how he'd reacted—

how worried he'd been about her health and the babies. "Can I ask you a question?"

He nodded.

"Did your wife have a hard time with her pregnancy?" The question hung in the air. But it was out there. No way to take it back. Even when she saw the telltale tick in his jaw muscle.

"She was miserable through the entire pregnancy."

Part of her didn't want to push but...part of her really wanted to know about the woman he'd been married to. "What was her name?"

He pushed out of his chair and crossed to the fire. The library fell eerily silent as he stared into the low-burning flames. All she could do was sit and stare at him. His rigid posture gave away his struggle. "Shanna."

Shanna. The mother of his son. His wife. Renata couldn't begin to imagine what she was like. Or how horrible it would be to lose the person you'd chosen to spend the rest of your life with. All she could do was sympathize with his grief. Her father had been distraught when her mother passed. It had taken him years to pull himself together. Meeting Clara had restored some of the pluck to his step and the sparkle to his eyes, but he still missed her mother.

Ash turned, his face cast in shadows. "Shanna was diagnosed with pancreatic cancer right after we discovered she was pregnant." There was no emotion in his voice. "She held on as long as she could, determined to meet him. But...she went into labor at thirty-three weeks." He sounded so empty, too hollow. "She went into a coma, and died a few months later."

Tears filled her eyes, the injustice of his words pressing in on her. And his pain? There was no escaping it. She was up, tripping over her blanket to get to him. Without hesitation or thought, she wrapped her arms around him, offering comfort he hadn't asked for but needed all the same. His arms slid around her waist and he held her flush against him, close enough to feel the rapid thump of his heart and the ragged hitch in his breath.

"She did get to meet him?" It was a whisper.

He buried his face against her neck and breathed deep. "Yes."

She sniffed, wiping her tears away but never letting him go. They stood, wrapped up and silent. The only sound was the crackle and pop from the fireplace and the steady thud of his heartbeat beneath her ear. She tried not to respond to his scent or the stroke of his hand along her back. Tried not to respond when his fingers ran through her hair. But when his nose traced along her neck and a shudder racked his body, there was no mistaking what was happening.

"I didn't come here to be seduced," she whispered. "Not this time."

His chuckle was low and breathy. "I didn't come here planning on seducing you." His lips brushed the shell of her ear. "But here we are." He tilted her head back, cradling her cheek in one hand. "And there's nothing I want more."

This close, it was impossible to miss the angry color along his jaw. "What happened to your face?" She knew, before the words were out, she knew. What the hell were they thinking? They were grown men, for crying out loud. "Which one of them—"

"It doesn't hurt. And, honestly, I deserved worse," he interrupted, pressing a soft, clinging kiss against her lips. "I knocked up his sister." His gaze fell to her lips. "And enjoyed doing it."

That look. That kiss. "You did?" She smiled.

"You doubt that?" His brow arched. "Let me convince you." Between the fire in his eyes and the burn building in her belly, it was hard to hold his gaze and breathe. He wanted her. She ached for him. All that was left was to kiss him.

So she did.

His fingers tightened in her hair, a soft moan spilling from his chest as his lips sealed with hers. On and on, his kiss clung and deepened. When his tongue dipped into her mouth, she swayed into the wall of his chest.

Need crashed into her.

Her hands had a mind of their own, trailing down his chest to free his shirt from the waist of his jeans. She wanted to touch him. Her fingers slid beneath the fabric to stroke the muscles of his abdomen. He shuddered, his skin contracting beneath her caress.

"Your hands are cold." He said against her mouth, laughing and arching away from her touch. His gaze swept over her face, a slight crease dipping between his dark brows before he reached for her again. Suddenly, Ash was urgent. Frantic. Impatient. His hands slid beneath her sweater, skimming the skin along her waistband and driving her wild. Need ruled him—and Renata welcomed it.

* * *

Ash had lost control. The minute he'd pulled her scent deep into his lungs, the red flag had popped up. But having her in his arms, soft and giving, was too much to resist. Hell, he didn't want to resist. He wanted to explore every inch of this woman, to love her until she fell apart, then do it all again. Knowing she felt the same—well, he was rock hard and hurting.

He let her go long enough to lock the large wooden door, but even that seemed to take too long. When he turned back to her, she stood before the glowing embers in the dying fire. He swallowed at the sight she made. That long blond hair of hers fell heavy down her back. Her jeans clung to her like a second skin. Only her bulky cream sweater left anything to the imagination. But he had no problem filling in the blanks. For weeks, Renata Boone had been waiting for him in his dreams. Now she was here, flesh and blood and wanting him.

"Ash…" Her voice wavered, uncertain, even as she held her hand out for him.

He kicked his boots off on the way to her, fingers unbuttoning his shirt as he went. She followed suit, sliding the sweater up and over her head and tossing it aside. Her navy bra was a stark contrast to her creamy skin. He wanted to push the straps aside to explore the full roundness of her breasts until she was writhing beneath him. Her gaze locked with his, wild-eyed and flushed, for him.

Once he reached her, clothes were flying. Her bare skin against his rocked him to the core. He lost himself in her, the silk of her skin and the scent that had haunted him since the night he'd first held her close. The nip in the air had him dragging her chair closer to the fire and warmth.

She smiled and pushed him back before climbing into his lap, straddling him.

He ran his fingers along her shoulder and chest, watching the dancing shadows flicker across her smooth skin. A long lock of hair fell forward, resting in the valley between her bare breasts. She was beautiful. Soft. She made him ache. When she bent to press her lips to his, his hands tangled in her hair—holding her close. But not close enough.

With a little groan of frustration, Renata arched into him. When her nipples grazed his chest, Ash bit off a curse. She braced her hands on his shoulders, broke away from their kiss and smiled down at him.

All he could do was stare. Hair tousled, eyes glazed with passion, lips parted… He knew what it was to love her, knew how it felt, and when she arched her hips and welcomed him deep inside her warmth nothing compared. His head pressed back against the chair as his lungs emptied. All that mattered was the feel of her, tight and hot, around him.

His hands gripped her hips, holding her in place once they'd fully joined together. "I need a minute," he ground out. Otherwise, this would be over way too soon.

She shook her head, tilting her hips ever so slightly. "Ash."

It was a plea. One he couldn't ignore. His hands traveled up her sides to cradle the weight of her full breasts.

The hard, tight peaks ached for him—so he bent forward to draw one, then the other, into his mouth. With every stroke of his tongue, she moaned a little harder, her grip on his shoulder a little tighter.

And every time she thrust onto him, he had to bite back a curse. Slow and hard, over and over, she didn't stop. Her head fell back so her long golden hair brushed his bare thighs. He captured a handful, tugging her close so he could bury his face between her breasts.

The moment her body began to tighten, he let go. He arched into her, letting her set the rhythm but matching it thrust for thrust. Her eyes flew open and she buried her face against his shoulder, muffling the long cry that signaled her release. That was all it took to send him spiraling over the edge. There was no way he could stop the groan that ripped from him.

She collapsed into him, burrowing close. Her slight shiver had him tugging the blanket up. Having her in his arms felt right. This felt right. Neither one of them could deny that this was powerful. Maybe powerful enough to bind them together—until affection kicked in.

He rubbed her back with long, slow strokes, listening as her breathing grew steady and she was relaxed in his hold.

"Renata?" he whispered.

"Hmm?" She glanced up at him, smiling. "You look pleased with yourself."

"After that? Hell, yes, I am." He grinned. "Watching you." He cleared his throat. "Pleasing you."

"You did. You do." She bit her lower lip, a shaky breath escaping. "You convinced me."

He ran his knuckles along her jaw, leisurely exploring the shape of her face. Holding her close, having her smile up at him like that, made everything fall into place. For one thing, there was *this*. The intensity of the fire between them was undeniable. But this, the tenderness she stirred in the sweet after, was just as intense.

Her brothers thought the world of her. His bruise seemed to satisfy them as a whole—which was a relief because his insides were still tender. They'd let him do most of the fence repairs while they discussed options on how he'd have the most luck winning her over. By the afternoon's end, all that had been decided was he needed luck because getting Renata Boone to change her mind was something rarely accomplished.

It was more than luck he needed. But admitting what was in his heart, right now, would have her running from the room—or throwing up all over him. Right now, he was pretty damn content.

"What are you thinking?" she asked.

Nothing she was ready to hear. Instead, he shrugged, smiling slowly.

Her brows rose, a mischievous sparkle in her eye. "Dr. Carmichael." She lowered her voice to a whisper. "Are you thinking sexy thoughts?" She bit her lower lip.

He hadn't been. But now… Her simple act of biting her lower lip sent his mind on a detour. His hand slid up, slowly, along her thigh to her hip. "Sexy thoughts? As in?"

She turned an adorable shade of red, still whispering, "All the things you want to do to me."

"You mean all the things you want me to do to you?" His fingers traced up her side, around her rib cage and up. His hand hovered, inches from her breast.

Her breathing picked up. "Maybe."

"Has to be your bed, considering mine probably has a toddler in it." He grinned. "What *you* have in mind might just take all night."

She was smiling again. "Mine. My apartment is downstairs—out of the way and quiet."

"Good." His thumb brushed the hardened tip of her nipple, causing her to arch into him. "You're noisy."

Her hand clasped his wrist and pulled his hand closer. "I'll bite the pillow," she gasped. "Since this is all about what I want… Kiss me."

He did, focusing entirely on the woman in his arms.

Chapter 12

"Check." Renata drew a line through the Ginger-bread Festival. What a festival it had been. Poor Ash might never recover. Still, he'd kept his cool, and no one—gingerbread houses included—had been injured in the judging process.

The Stonewall Crossing High School Ag Club had won. And while three long-standing competitors and previous winners had argued and questioned the decision, the judges didn't budge. And the kids were ecstatic. She didn't know what made them happier, bragging rights or the five-hundred-dollar prize that went to the winner. Either way, the town had been pleased when the kids' names were called out—silencing any further protests from their competitors.

"Tomorrow is the Christmas parade and then it's

Christmas Eve, babies. Then we're taking a vacation."
She ran her hand over the slightest swell of her stomach. "Your mom needs a vacation."

As if the stress of the holiday season and the Gingerbread Festival hadn't been enough, she'd had to grin and bear many a question about Ash Carmichael, her pregnancy and their impending engagement. Lucky for her, she had allies. Between her sisters-in-law and, surprisingly, the mothers, Renata had managed to escape before questioning turned truly invasive.

Overall, it had been a good week. The more time she spent with Curtis, the more in love she fell. His easy nature and quick smile were impossible to resist. He was a mini-Ash, all dimples and charm. And the mothers? Well, they were hysterical. She looked forward to them playing just as big a role in her children's lives as they were doing for Curtis.

Ash did his part to make the week pretty incredible, too. He managed to sneak in at least a dozen stolen kisses, several lingering touches and one night of invigorating lovemaking, followed by whispering in her bed into the wee hours of the morning. If there had been any remaining doubts about her feelings for the man, they were gone. She loved him. Unconditionally.

And it had to stop.

But he was making that impossible.

Her desk phone buzzed. "Miss Boone, there's a delivery for you." Irma sounded delighted.

She glanced at the clock. Right before lunch. "Coming." The same time, every day for the last four days, Ash had sent her a surprise. After she opened one, he'd call and they'd have lunch. When it was just the two of them, the intimacy felt real and promising. But this whole public display of whatever this was made her nervous. Was he still planning something calamitous—like he had at Archer's ball? The pressure he was under, as an outsider, was incredible. If he buckled, could she blame him?

Yes, she could. He knew how she felt about marrying without love. And this, the presents and the lunches and the smiles and the touches, only toyed with her heart and weakened her resolve to hold out for the real thing.

Not that the surprises were in any way romantic. They were…interesting. Ash had a unique sense of humor. One more thing to love about him.

As if I needed something else.

Surprise one, a picture of a partridge badly photoshopped into a pear tree, sat in the bookcase opposite her desk. Quirky as it was, Renata loved it.

A carved wooden ornament, two turtledoves beak-to-beak, was day two.

Her coffee cup rested on day three's surprise: a ceramic coaster, painted with three hens in berets.

Day four, he'd sent her four wind-up birds. They hobbled around, stopped, opened their wings and made the most horrible grating sound she'd ever heard. She'd burst out laughing but vowed never, ever, to wind them up again. If she were smart, she'd put them someplace her nieces and nephews couldn't reach or they'd be squawking all the time.

Day five meant…rings.

She paled, eyeing the box the delivery man carried into her office with apprehension. A small box. Rings. Engagements. Nausea. And…hope.

Damn you, Ash Carmichael.

Renata opened the box, fighting back excitement as she sifted through the tissue paper inside. Until she saw what he'd sent.

"Teething rings." A nervous giggle erupted. This was good. A relief. A huge relief. So why didn't she feel that way?

"Really?" Irma asked, peeking her head in the door. "Well, that's… Huh."

She held the teething rings for Irma's inspection. "It's the most practical gift so far." Which was true, but that didn't stop a knot from lodging in her throat.

Irma's eyes narrowed, then widened. "There's only four." She practically ran into the office, making a bee-line for the box on Renata's desk.

Renata glared at her, but Irma was already picking up the box and shaking it. Sure enough, something else was inside. The lump in her throat doubled in size as Irma smiled and offered the box back.

No. Renata eyed the box. She didn't want to know what was inside. She really didn't. But she was turning over the box, dumping the cotton padding onto her desk… A gold key ring. With a key on it. She blew out a slow, deep breath.

Her phone rang.

"Hello?" she asked, turning the key over.

"You get it?" It was Ash.

She cleared her throat. "Yes. Ash, thank you. But this has to stop, really. I'm not sure why—"

"You're not curious?"

She turned the key over. "Fine. Yes. What is it?"

He chuckled. "I'm outside. Let's go try out the key."

"Okay. Give me a minute." She tucked the teething rings and key ring into her purse, slipped into her coat and hurried down the hall.

"Enjoy your lunch." Irma waved.

The urge to climb into his lap and shower him with very thorough, very passionate kisses was there—like it had been for the past four days. But he wasn't alone. The mothers and Curtis were in the truck waiting.

"Hi, everybody." She climbed into Ash's truck and reached back to squeeze Curtis's foot. Curtis squealed in reply.

"Let's go." Ash chuckled before turning the truck and heading back down Main Street.

"Guess I can't ask where we're going?" She glanced his way.

He winked. "You can ask."

She shook her head, grinning like a fool.

"Set us straight, Renata," Nancy Carmichael said. "Is the big parade tonight or tomorrow?"

"Tomorrow," she said, playing peekaboo with Curtis over the back of her seat. "You ready to meet Santa Claus?"

Curtis's little feet kicked and he babbled with great enthusiasm.

"I thought so," she agreed, wiggling his little foot and smiling.

"It's awful cold. We'll have to bundle him up so he doesn't catch pneumonia." Betty said. "He doesn't have much in the way of winter clothing."

Which reminded her. "I meant to tell you earlier—Kylee and Annabeth have boxes of clothes for Curtis. And toys. If you don't mind hand-me-downs?"

"Why would I mind?" Ash asked, his deep voice making her insides melt a little more.

They'd left town and were heading toward her family's ranch—but he passed the gate and kept right on going.

"That's where we met," he interrupted Betty and Nancy's back seat debate on which laundry detergent irritated Curtis's skin and pointed out the window.

Renata looked past him at the stretch of fence line. He was right. She could never have anticipated how much that dreamy-eyed photographer would change her life.

"There?" Betty asked. "On the side of the road? Were you hitchhiking?"

"My rental truck broke down," he explained. "Renata rode up on her horse and rescued me."

She laughed. "Is that what happened?"

He shot her a look. "I like my version."

"Whatever happened, it turned out just fine." His mother reached forward to pat Ash on the shoulder. "My son is smiling again. What more could a mother ask for?"

Renata's heart thumped against her rib cage. He did seem happier—maybe. Or was that what she wanted to see? Still, he winked when she glanced his way. That wink, that smile, kicked up the molten burn only Ash Carmichael stirred. She was so distracted, she didn't realize where they were until he'd parked in front of Gruber House. He sat back, watching her.

"The key?" she asked.

He nodded. "Signed everything this morning."

The mothers were already climbing out of the truck, taking Curtis with them, but Renata didn't move. "Ash. Why are you giving me a key?"

"I'm hoping you'll want to spend a lot of time here. I like the Lodge and I respect it's your home, but it's not my home. And, honestly, I can't imagine raising Curtis and the twins there." He cleared his throat. "Space, I think you said? Plenty of that here. And a home. For whatever happens next."

Her happiness fizzled. *We*—he and Curtis and the twins. She was welcome here, anytime, but the Lodge was her home. Last time he'd mentioned this place, he'd teased her about the kids they'd have in the future. Not this time. Instead, he was following her rules and using her terms. *Space. Whatever happens next.* None of that had to mean something bad. Something like Ash finding his soul mate and moving into her dream house to have the half a dozen kids he'd teased her about. Talk about going to extremes… Her overactive imagination had doubled since she'd gotten pregnant—which only amped up her emotional seesaw.

"We should probably open the place up before they freeze." He pointed at the mothers, leaning over hedges to peer inside.

She nodded, climbed out of the truck and opened the

front door. Betty and Nancy took off, opening doors and shouting back and forth about every little detail. There was good reason to be excited. Everything was pretty…perfect. The more she saw, the easier it was to envision living here, and the harder it was not to cry. She carried Curtis upstairs, peering into each room she passed. It was the last room on the left that made her pause.

A nursery. The palest mint green with detailed white trim. Massive windows and a wide window seat peered out into the overgrown garden behind the house. Beyond that, the pastures, a small fruit orchard and bare grape vines promised an incredible spring view. Sitting here, in a rocking chair, singing lullabies and reading books.

"What do you think?" she whispered to Curtis.

He was sound asleep in her arms. She buried her nose against his glossy black curls.

This, all of this, was everything she'd ever wanted. Well, most of it.

Was it too late to tell him she'd marry him? To settle for what he would give her versus what she truly wanted? He'd do it, she knew he would. And she'd have him, forever. But the thought of trapping him in a loveless marriage… No, that was wrong—for both of them.

Seeing her in the nursery, holding Curtis close… If the words hadn't clogged up his throat, he'd have told her how he felt. Loving her wasn't a choice. It was a truth. A truth he worried she wouldn't believe.

"What do you think?" His voice was gruff, hoarse.

She turned, facing him, and his heart clamped down—hard.

"It's a great house." Her eyes darted away. "Just like I remembered it."

Something was wrong. Her smile wasn't quite right. With Renata, her smile lit her up from the inside. It was warm and real, making her eyes shine and his burdens ease. The exact opposite of how he was feeling now, when her smile was tight and forced and her eyes were pointedly avoiding his.

"What's up?" he asked, stepping forward.

She shook her head.

"Why won't you look at me?" he pushed.

She rolled her incredible blue eyes and stared at him. "Happy?"

The sheen in her eyes was a kick in the gut. Hell, no, he wasn't happy. What was wrong? "Renata—"

"I need to get back, Ash," she cut him off. "The parade is tomorrow—"

"I know." He sighed. "And I know, from Irma, that you've checked and rechecked every tiny detail."

Her gaze fell from his. "I still need to get back." She shifted Curtis, her nose brushing his dark curls. "Please."

She could dodge him now. The excited chatter of the mothers was growing closer anyway. And Curtis needed his nap. But she couldn't avoid him forever— he'd make damn sure of that. "Fine. But we're getting you something to eat."

She glared at him. "*Someone* had a ham and cheese *kolache* delivered to the office this morning."

He glared right back. "A *kolache* you should have eaten for breakfast."

"Ash…" She broke off, sucking in a deep breath, meeting his gaze. "We need to talk."

A coldness seeped in, starting at the top of his head and descending slowly southward. "Talk." He forced the word out.

She pressed her eyes shut. "Fine. Please stop. Please." She buried her nose in Curtis's hair. "I know you're going to be a good father—you already are. But you? And me? We both know we're playing with fire acting this way."

He stepped closer, hating the gulf widening between them.

Her gaze darted to his. "I'm pregnant. My emotions are in overdrive. By the time I've sifted through what I'm feeling, it's changed." She swallowed. "Being attracted to me isn't a valid reason to marry me. Getting me pregnant isn't a valid reason to marry me—no matter what you or my father think. Only love, Ash. We both know there's no way a person can fall in love so soon." Her posture stiffened. "Just, please, stop with the presents, the lunches, the…gestures. All of it. You're sending mixed signals."

He had to try. "I wasn't trying to—"

"You are. The whole town thinks you're courting me." She shook her head, her voice rising enough for Curtis to stir. "But we both know you're *not*. I'm not sure why you're doing what you're doing. Maybe you're feeling the pressure from…everyone. Maybe you still believe I can't do this on my own—"

"I never said that." His hands rested on her shoulders, needing her warmth to chase off the coldness that seeped into his bones.

"Maybe…" She swallowed. "Maybe it's because of your wife?" Her eyes met his. "I'm healthy, Ash. I'm going to be fine. I know you've been to hell and back." She cleared her throat. "What's happening here is different. It's not real. It's based on heightened emotion and wildly out-of-control desire. It can't end well. It would be nice for us to stay friends while we're raising our children." She stumbled over the last words. "This needs to stop before people get hurt."

What the hell could he say to that? How could he argue?

Not real?

Meaning she didn't love him. Whatever he thought or felt didn't matter. She wouldn't marry without love— it wasn't enough that he loved her.

She left him standing in the nursery, numb and desperate and scrambling for some way to make this better. All the way back to town, he was sifting through her words—needing something to hold on to, some glimmer of hope that he, and his heart, still had a chance with her.

"Thanks for the adventure." She smiled into the back seat before sliding from the truck cab and hurrying inside the City Offices.

He sat, staring at the door, his hands tightening around the steering wheel. That was it? She'd said what she needed to say and that was that? That wasn't how this was going to work. He didn't think through what he'd say or do before he mumbled, "Be back," and followed her inside.

He nodded at Irma and headed straight to Renata's office, closing the door behind them before she could argue.

"Ash?" She sniffed, her attempt to shrug out of her coat frozen as she stared at him.

The sight of her tear-filled eyes had him crossing the floor, the numbness giving way to something sharp and cutting. "I don't get a say in any of this?"

She shook her head, wiping her eyes.

"No?" he bit out, searching her face, stepping closer. The words were there—all he had to do was say them. But she'd made it clear she wouldn't believe him. How could he love her after a couple of weeks? How could he know he wanted to spend the rest of his life with her? All he knew was he did. Even if she didn't feel the same way. "How's that fair?"

"None of this is fair, Ash." Her gaze fell to his lips. "None of it. But you know I'm right."

A hard, short snort escaped, frustration and anger kicking in. She wasn't willing to love him, to let him love her, but she wanted him. And, dammit, he ached for her. To be close to her. To touch her. He'd take what he could get. "I know you want me to kiss you."

She was still staring at his mouth, her cheeks flushing. "I'll get over it."

It hurt to breathe. "And I want to kiss you." He cradled her cheek.

Her eyes met his, her teeth sinking into her lower lip as she leaned into his palm. "This is the last time—"

He pressed her against the wall, hands cradling her face as his mouth lowered to hers. It was a long and slow kiss, his lips sealing with hers and breathing her in—searing her scent and taste and feel into his fingertips and tongue.

She clung, swaying into him as her arms wound around his neck and her fingers slid through his hair. Her hunger rolled over him, giving him permission to deepen the kiss for a moment longer. Didn't she feel this? Know that this wasn't just attraction but something more. Something real.

With a groan, he tore his mouth from hers and stared down at her. How he managed to let her go, to step back, and have the icy void slide between them, he didn't know. But he had to leave before he said or did something he'd regret. "You might get over wanting this. I'm not so sure I will."

He could have stayed there, lost in her blue eyes—hoping she'd change her mind. But loving her meant wanting her happiness and that meant leaving. Every step away from her was a struggle.

Chapter 13

"Next we have the Stonewall Crossing Trail Riders." Quinton Sheehan spoke into the microphone.

"This group will be making a trip to the Rocky Mountains this summer for a competitive trail riding competition," Lola chimed in. "They're looking for sponsors to make this trip a reality."

"Well, I'll be." Quinton nudged Renata, hard. "Tell us how the fine folk can help?"

Renata blinked. "Right." She stared at the words on the white index card. "It says here that each horse has two battery packs wired into the wreath it's wearing."

Lola and Quinton were staring at her.

"Pregnancy brain," he whispered.

Lola chuckled.

She ignored them. "And…did you know braiding a mane can take a couple of hours?"

Quinton spoke into his mic. "Why, no, Renata, I didn't know that."

Lola covered her microphone. "He asked about sponsorship information, sweetie."

Renata forced a smile. "If you're interested in sponsoring this wonderful group of young people, touch base with George Rios or Monica Castillo." She read off the rest of the card and eyed the remaining stack of cards. The parade had barely started and she was already wishing it was over.

So far, her co-commentators had landed a good dozen pregnancy and/or engagement digs, and they'd only been sitting on the stage for forty minutes.

"Let's all give this fine group a wave." Lola spoke. "Oh my, next up is Dr. Farriday's Christmas float. Look at that."

Renata glanced up. There, pulled behind a diesel pickup, was Dr. Farriday's float. A massive baby cradle made of papier-mâché, pink and blue streamers, and lights rocked—yes, rocked—on the flatbed trailer where it rested.

"Isn't that the sweetest thing?" Lola asked, reaching over Quinton to pat her arm. "This time next year, you'll be rocking your own cradles, Renata."

There were more than a few laughs from the crowd.

"Two cradles," Quinton sounded off. "You'll have your hands full."

Renata cut them off, reading the neatly printed information off the card she held.

"Dr. Farriday and her staff wish you all a very happy and healthy holiday," Quinton added. "And we want to thank her for being one of tonight's sponsors."

"Next up, we have a team from Boone Lodge pulling a festive hayride," Lola said, waving.

A hayride she wished she was a part of.

Still, she was proud of her father, sitting tall in the driver's seat of his prized wagon. And in the back? Her nieces and nephews all but overflowed the wagon, waving and blowing kisses her way as they made their way down the parade route and past the stage.

"How many grandchildren do you have now, Teddy?" Quinton called out.

"Not near enough," her father called back, tipping his hat and shooting her a wink.

Quinton laughed, and so did Lola—but she winced, waiting.

"Well, you'll have two more before you know it." Lola shot her a look. "First things first, when's that boy going to propose?"

"Can't blame him for being gun-shy. We all know what happened last time he tried." Quinton was chuckling.

That chuckle was beginning to wear on her nerves. Nerves that had been shot since Ash had kissed her in her office.

"Renata?" Lola prodded.

"Yes?" she asked, glancing at the older woman all decked out like Mrs. Claus.

"I asked who was next, dear." She gave her a sympathetic click.

"Next we have the Stonewall Crossing Quilting Guild." She read the card with as much enthusiasm as she could muster. There was no way they could tie this float into her pregnancy or nonengagement.

"We'll have to see about getting them to work on a wedding-ring quilt for you and Dr. Carmichael." Lola waved. "What do you think, ladies?"

"Already started," Nancy Guerra called back. "And Tiffy's started working on quilts for the twins, too."

Renata slumped forward. This was torture. It couldn't get any worse—

"Next up, we have riders from the University of East Texas Veterinary Teaching Hospital's large animal clinic," Quinton boomed. "Why, look there, if it isn't your beau in the saddle."

Of course it was. Renata didn't want to look. She really didn't. But, somehow, her gaze found him.

Eventually, she'd see him and her heart wouldn't seize up like this. He'd always be handsome, there was no way around that. But her feelings would fade. This horrible pain would fade. She had to believe that.

His gaze bounced her way. The instant tightening of his jaw wreaked havoc on her pulse.

"Why, Dr. Carmichael, I bet Teddy Boone has his shotgun loaded and ready." Lola was teasing—and the crowd loved it. "Should we expect a Christmas wedding?"

Renata wasn't sure what was worse, the sweat breaking out on her brow and upper lip or the sudden churning of her stomach.

"No, ma'am." Quinton shook his head. "I'm guessing you're planning something big?" He looked at her.

She sipped her water, hoping it would settle her stomach. "No."

Lola and Quinton both looked her way.

"No?" Lola asked. "Something smaller? Well, that makes sense. Considering."

Renata ran a hand over her face, willing her stomach to behave. Now was the perfect time to set everyone—*everyone*—straight. She glanced up, only to realize Ash had reined his horse in and sat directly in front of the stage.

"Well, well, Dr. Carmichael looks like he has something to say." Lola's excitement was tangible.

In fact, a ripple of excitement seemed to spill out over the crowd.

But Renata had never seen that look before. Ash was…angry. Really angry.

"Um, Lola." Quinton must have picked up on Ash's mood.

"Hush now, Quinton, this is the most excitement this parade's ever had." She clapped her hands together.

Ash looked about ready to explode.

Renata stood. "No one's proposing tonight. At least, not here. No one's getting married. And, even though you all have very particular opinions on my personal life, I'd like to put this matter to rest. Ash has asked me to marry him. But I said no. Now, how about we get back to what matters and greet the next group…" She ignored Ash and Lola and Quinton and glanced at her card. "A dance troupe all the way from Austin. Clogging, I believe that's what it's called?"

It took the other two a minute to pick back up where they'd left off, but once they did she handed the mic to Quinton and left the stage.

Ash wasn't mad. He was furious. He didn't give a damn about how the town of Stonewall Crossing felt about him—not after that little display. But Renata? That they'd publicly humiliate her that way?

He fumed for the rest of the parade, did his best not to snap while getting the horses loaded for their ride back to Archer's place and tried to smile for Curtis when Santa rode into town on the last float of the night.

"You look like a thundercloud," his mother whispered as they drove the long road back to the Lodge.

"Feel like one," he answered.

"Can't say that I blame you." She patted his arm. "I've never… Well, I've never."

He nodded.

"What are you going to do?"

He glanced at his mother. "Check on her. See what she needs."

She studied him. "You going to tell her you love her, Ash?"

He shook his head. "If I thought she'd believe me. Right now, she's too wary of another obligatory proposal."

"Maybe if she heard it, often and regularly, she would." She sat back against the leather passenger seat.

"She said she needed space." He cleared his throat. "Said this couldn't end well between us."

She sighed. "You young people make everything so hard. All these rules and expectations just get in the way. Betty and I were talking to Clara—"

"Oh, here we go." He chuckled. "I can't wait to hear this."

"Shush now." She placed a hand on his arm. "We're old, yes, because we have more experience. And all that experience might just mean we have, occasionally, some words of wisdom to impart."

"I'm all ears." He and his mother had been a team long before Shanna came into his life. She was the only other constant in his world and she deserved his respect—even if he didn't always agree with her advice.

"If those babies weren't coming, would you be courting her?" She waited, arms crossed over her chest.

"Yes."

"You didn't have to think that through much." His mother sounded delighted.

"Nope." He glanced her way. "I'm not saying I'd be proposing already but...eventually, yeah."

"Then tell her that." She smiled. "Start there."

If only it were that easy. But he nodded, parking in front of the Lodge and turning off the engine.

"Better make it quick, Ash." His mother's voice was tight.

He looked out the passenger window to see Renata's yellow truck, the doors open and the toolbox wide—a suitcase on the ground beside it. She was leaving. Again.

"Dammit," he ground out.

"You can hardly blame her." His mother patted his arm. "You go on. I'll get Curtis. Just remember, this is hard on her, too."

He nodded before climbing from the truck, all the carefully planned words he'd come up with on the drive here evaporating the closer he got to her vehicle.

The gravel crunched under his boots, alerting her to his arrival. He didn't miss the way she ran her hand over her long braid or the deep breath she took before she faced him.

"I'm not in the mood, Ash. I'm leaving in the morning," she snapped, avoiding his gaze. "No lecture needed."

"No lecture." He leaned against the truck, watching her.

Her eyes met his, brows rising in question.

The cold had the tip of her nose and her cheeks bright red. And he'd never seen a prettier sight. "Worried is more like it," he admitted.

Her gaze fell, her tone brittle. "They meant well."

"Renata." He tapped his fingers along the truck bed. "I've been reeling since yesterday. Trying to figure out what to say and how to say it."

"After tonight, no one will say a thing about us getting married." She shrugged, dismissive. If it wasn't for the irritation rolling off her, he might have bought it.

But he was irritated, too. "I don't give a shit about what these people say or think, not after tonight."

He had her attention then. Those eyes were fixed on him. The hint of a smile on her lips. And damn, she was beautiful. "There's nothing left to say." Beautiful and stubborn.

"Wrong." He stepped closer. "I have plenty to say."

She stood her ground, a hint of defiance in the tilt of her chin. "I need a break, Ash." Her gaze fell to his mouth, briefly.

"Space." He ground the word out. "I know. I'm trying." Even if it was the last thing he wanted.

"Really?" She crossed her arms over her chest, tucking her hands against her sides. "Try harder."

"You don't own gloves?" he asked, spying her bare hands. "It's below freezing, Renata."

"Stop it." Her calm vanished. "Stop pretending you care about me. I'm not your responsibility."

He froze, her words a shock. "I didn't mean it that way—"

"I'm not going to risk these babies, ever. They're mine. I love them. And they will love me—" Her voice broke.

"I know that." He spoke softly. He would love her if she'd let him—if she'd listen. "I need to tell you something, okay? Can you—"

"Wh-why won't you leave me alone?" Her voice rose.

"How can I leave you alone and be here for our family? I can't. I won't. I'm not going anywhere. When you get back, I'll be here, waiting."

She was shaking her head. "Great. Wonderful." She slammed her truck door. "Just, please, leave me alone *now*. Let me have time to get over you—over this—so it doesn't hurt to see you. You're always there… Always. Is that asking too much? For you to stop being there when I turn around?"

Each word crashed into him. *Over him. Hurt to see him…* Words that caused her pain and gave him hope. Had she just said what he hoped she'd said? He reached for her then. "Renata—"

"No, Ash." She stepped back, hands out in front of her.

"You realize you're yelling?" Fisher called from the front porch. "And our guests are complaining."

"Perfect." She spun, her braid flying. "Don't even think about following me."

He'd let her go, for now. And he wouldn't smile. Not now, when she was so upset. But dammit, he couldn't stop himself.

Chapter 14

"You got everything you need?" her father asked, tipping his hat back.

She nodded. "You don't need to drive me, Dad."

"I want to, long as you don't mind the detour?"

She shook her head. Fisher said a neighbor had called about a downed gate. Since they were closest, they'd check it out, let Fisher know and hit the road.

"Don't like the idea of you making the drive on your own. Awful lot of highway. I know you're anxious to see your cousins, but you said Tandy and Click are coming home for New Year's so they can bring you back." He glanced at her. "You are coming back?"

She swallowed. "I am."

"Promise?" His voice was soft, unsteady.

"I promise, Dad." She nodded.

"Sure wish you were waiting till after the holidays to go, Renata. This is the first Christmas without you."

She bit into her lower lip to hide the tremor.

"Last night was bad, I'm not going to lie," he grumbled. "And I gave Lola a talking-to—I don't care how bowed up her husband got. That woman needs to learn that she doesn't have to say every thought that goes through her brain."

She smiled. "She can't help it."

"She needs to try," he barked, reaching across the seat to take her hand. "That Sheehan fella should thank his stars Ash stopped Fisher from throwing a punch."

"He did?"

He nodded. "Good damn thing, too, or the fool would have ended up in the hospital—and your brother would probably be locked in a cell."

"He was that upset?" She wasn't the only one who had been humiliated last night. Her actions had reflected on her whole family.

"I haven't seen him like that since…ever." He shot her a look. "You okay?"

She nodded, his question making her eyes burn. Her gaze wandered out the window and over the winter landscape. A slight freeze covered the gray-brown grass. Was she okay? No. Not at all. She'd told Ash she cared about him—in a roundabout sort of tirade—but she'd said it. And he hadn't come after her. The one time she'd wanted him to come after her and he'd listened.

But if he had come after her, then what? They would have ended up in bed together and her heart would be more shattered than ever. He didn't love her. Period.

The sooner she accepted that, the sooner she could let go and move on.

"You don't look okay." His hand squeezed hers.

"I will be." She tried to smile.

His vibrant blue eyes, so like her own, narrowed. "It's that boy? Ash? He do something wrong?"

She stared down at their hands. As close as they were, she rarely bared her soul to her father. "Dad—"

"Don't you *Dad* me, Renata Jean. If your brothers and I need to—"

"Dad! No. Leave him alone. Please." She cut him off. "He hasn't done anything."

"Then why are you crying?" he asked, pulling his handkerchief from his shirt pocket.

"I'm not crying." She dabbed away the tears, sniffing fiercely.

"Come on now. You know I can't stand by and watch my girl cry." He caught her hand again.

"He didn't do anything. He proposed, I said no. Because he doesn't love me." She sniffed, wiping frantically at the tears that were streaming down her face. "And there's nothing anyone can do about that."

"Then the boy's a fool," he ground out, squeezing her hand. "He didn't strike me as a fool."

She shook her head. "He's not." The tears kept coming. "He's a good guy. A keeper." She gave up then, covering her face with her father's handkerchief and sobbing.

Minutes later, the truck rolled to a stop.

"Renata Jean. Give me a second?"

She nodded, staring at the handkerchief in her hands. "I'm sorry, Dad. For acting this way—"

"Nothing to apologize for, you hear me?" He smiled at her. "Your momma told me sometimes a good cry could make her feel better."

She laughed. "Let's hope so."

He nodded and climbed out of the truck.

It took a minute for her to realize where they were. They weren't at the gate. Not anywhere near the gate. They were in the heart of the ranch. At the vow tree.

She sat forward, peering through the windshield at her father. And her brothers. All gathered under the vow tree, talking to—

"Ash?"

What the hell was he doing here? Why was her father laughing? And her brothers?

"What is happening?" She pushed the truck door open, winced from the cold air and hurried toward her father, her brothers, Ash and the massive tree.

"Hi." Ash was smiling at her. That smile. The one that made her knees weak. And made her heart thump. And made her cheeks flush.

"Don't *hi* me," she managed. "I thought we were checking on a gate. For you." She faced Fisher, scowling. "What's going on?"

Her brothers were all smiles.

"We're heading out." Hunter walked off in the opposite direction, his truck parked, almost hidden, behind the tree break. Beside Ash's.

"Fisher?" she asked, hoping her twin would clue her in.

Instead, he shrugged and followed her other brothers to Hunter's truck.

"I'll leave you to it?" her father asked.

She frowned at her father. "Leave me?"

Her father held her by the shoulders. "I told you the boy wasn't a fool, Renata. Listen to him, would you?" With a parting nod at Ash, he headed back to his truck.

Her curiosity was rapidly turning into irritation. "I'm supposed to listen to you?" she asked, steeling herself to face him. She wouldn't let his smile or his dimples or the crinkles at the corners of his eyes disarm her. Until she faced him. And she reacted like she always did—uncontrollably. "I'm listening."

He nodded, his smile growing. "First, I got you something." He held out a package. "Curtis might have helped me wrap it."

She eyed the present. "I thought we said no more presents."

"You said no more presents, Renata." He pressed the crudely wrapped package into her hands.

She frowned, tearing the wrapping apart. And laughed. "Gloves."

He laughed, too. "You can put them on now."

With a shake of her head, she tugged on the down-lined leather gloves. "Okay. Happy?"

"Not yet." He reached up to tuck her hair behind her ear. "I can't give you space. I don't want you getting over me. Not now, not ever. I don't know how seeing me hurts you. All I know is not seeing you hurts me." His gray eyes wandered over her face. "Even if you weren't having my babies, we'd wind up here."

"What?" She shook her head. "I'm not sure—"

"I am. I love you. I am in love with you. I can't tell

you when it happened, only that it did. It's real. It's strong. And it's forever. Whether or not you marry me, I love you."

For the first time in her life, Renata Boone was completely speechless.

He blew out a slow breath. "Meeting you." He broke off and moved closer, wanting to touch her but knowing the spark between them would complicate things. "I missed my plane."

"What?" she frowned. "In October."

"I stood there, wondering what the hell had happened. You made me feel things I shouldn't be feeling—not yet, anyway. But I couldn't go. If Betty hadn't called, snapped me out of it, I might not have left." He shook his head. "Once I had, I didn't want to come back. Ever."

"I don't understand."

"You scared me." He swallowed. "After losing Shanna, I didn't want to be in that position again."

A tear hung from her long lashes then fell down her cheek.

"Fate brought me back, I believe that. I was supposed to come back because you were here. Maybe I was already a little in love with you then. It took everything I had to resist." He reached for her hand. He squeezed her fingers, breathing easier when she squeezed back. "I love you. I love the way you smile, the way you laugh, the way you love my son—and me. Even if you did insist on telling me everything I never wanted to know about the place I know is my home, I can't imagine my world without you."

She wiped the tears from her cheek.

"Tell me what to do now. Whatever you need, whatever I need to do, tell me."

"Say it again," she whispered.

"I love you," he whispered. "Forever."

He waited, breathless. The longer she stared at him, the more terrified he grew.

Her big blue eyes never wavered, searching, doubtful. "You're serious?" she whispered.

He nodded.

"This isn't about my family or—"

He shook his head. "This is me. Loving you. Hoping like hell I didn't just send you running for the hills." He groaned. "I know you might not feel the same way. Like you said, who falls in love in a few weeks—"

"I do," she whispered.

He could breathe again. "Pregnancy hormones?" His fingers brushed along her cheek.

"Possibly."

"I'll risk it," he murmured.

"Seeing you only hurt because it reminded me of what I wanted—but couldn't have." The hitch in her voice shook him to the core.

He closed the distance between them, wrapping his arms around her and resting his forehead against hers. "I'm yours, whether you want me or not. I'm done."

She smiled, tears running down her face. "I don't know why I'm crying. I can't stop crying."

"Happy tears?" he asked, tilting her face back. "I hope?"

Her nod was quick. "Are you happy now?"

He grinned. "Almost."

"Almost?" She shook her head. "What else could you want, Asher Carmichael?"

"For you to take off your left glove," he murmured, dropping to his knees before her.

"It's freezing," she argued.

"Then you'd better hurry up." He nodded at her gloved hand.

She tugged off the glove, more tears falling.

He lifted her hand and pressed it against his face. Her sweet scent filled his nostrils, soothing the ache deep inside and the hole in his heart. "Marry me, please, Renata. I want to wake up beside you and fall asleep in your arms. I want to laugh with you and cry with you—and *be* with you."

"Yes," she whispered. "Yes. I'll marry you." She tugged. "Now get up, please. Before you get pneumonia."

He stood, kissing her softly. "Glad you said yes." He pointed at the tree. "Since I already sort of committed us."

Her blue eyes searched the trunk until she found the fresh carving. RB + AC in a heart.

"Your dad says this is the best way to guarantee a long and happy marriage." He held her close. "That's all I want for us."

"This is real?" she whispered. "You mean this?"

"I mean it. I love you, Renata. And I'll happily spend the rest of my life making sure you believe me."

Chapter 15

"You didn't have to do this." Renata hugged Lola then Carl Stephens. Not that it surprised her in the least.

"We did, sweetie," Lola argued. "I'm ashamed of myself. Ashamed, you hear me?"

"Well, no, it all turned out fine," Carl finished. "More than fine."

"And it means so much to Ash and me." Renata eyed the wedding cake Lola and Carl had made for them. Considering she and Ash had pulled the ceremony together in two days, it was coming out quite nicely. The three-tier, lacy-iced confection was gorgeous. "It's truly beautiful. And I know it will taste even better." Hopefully, she'd be able to enjoy a piece. After all, it was her wedding day.

"Let's hope so. It's not every day we have something

this special to celebrate." Lola waved aside her arguments. "This is the last Boone wedding."

"Come on, Lola, this girl's gotta go get hitched," Carl said, patting Renata's cheek. "We'll see you at Cutter's for the party later on."

To say their wedding reception would be nontraditional was an understatement. But once word had spread that they were getting married, the whole town had stepped in to help—day after Christmas or not. And since the wedding wasn't going to be a big affair, the reception had to make up for it. Her brothers, their wives and who knew who else had been drafted into helping put together this last-minute reception party, had been up since before dawn getting ready. The Lodge was at capacity and, considering the number of people expected at the reception, was too small a venue anyway. Cutter's was a pool hall, but they'd open up the dance hall so there'd be plenty of room. Added good news—she and Ash might be able to sneak away without staying until the wee hours of the morning.

But first, she had to get married.

"Renata?" Fisher cleared his throat. "You ready?"

She nodded, beyond excited to be marrying Ash Carmichael. She'd imagined, once or twice, what it would be like to be loved by him. But her imagination hadn't come close. He loved with abundance.

"You look beautiful." There were tears in her brother's eyes, a rarity. "I know I punched him and all, but I like him well enough. But, you know, if he ever messes up…"

"I know." She stood on tiptoe and kissed his cheek.

"And I'm pretty sure Ash knows. But he won't. Don't worry."

"I'm not." He smiled a wobbly smile. "I want you to be happy. Always."

"Then don't you dare cry." She wiped at his eye. "I'm the emotional one. Remember?"

"Yeah, yeah." He sniffed.

Laughter bubbled up. At the end of the day, he'd always be her overprotective brother, willing to punch first and ask questions later. It helped to know that Ash would never do anything that would land him at the end of her brother's fists. "Let's go."

"Yes, ma'am." He chuckled, hooked her arm through his and led her out to his truck. She let him help her into the passenger seat, then smoothed the white lace fabric over her legs. Eden had insisted Renata wear her wedding dress. It was simple and elegant—just like Eden. The tea-length dress had a full bell skirt, extensive lacework and delicate beading around the sweetheart neckline. It was a little snug on her belly and a little short, but Renata felt pretty anyway. And, as Eden pointed out, it was her something borrowed.

She'd considered the selection of heels and pumps her sisters-in-law had rounded up, but none of them worked. Instead, she'd slipped on her favorite pair of embroidered ostrich-skin boots. After a long debate on what to do with her hair, she'd put her booted foot down. Ash liked her hair and she was leaving it down.

Her sisters-in-law had the whole wedding luck thing covered. A blue silk garter for something blue. Her engagement ring—something old. And the strand of pearls her father had left wrapped for her under the Christmas tree was her something new.

But she and Ash wouldn't need much luck. They had love.

The drive to town had never been so quick. Kylee and Josie rode with her and Fisher, filling the otherwise silent drive by sharing stories about the kids, their favorite Christmas gifts, the newest recipes that were a hit, and a handful of pregnancy tips Renata was too distracted to remember. When they parked in front of the small whitewashed building that was City Hall, Renata all but jumped out of the truck.

"Careful." Kylee laughed. "He's not going anywhere, believe me."

"He's right where he wants to be." Josie pressed a kiss against her cheek.

Her father was waiting for her outside the front door. "You make the prettiest bride I've ever seen, Renata Boone. Your momma is smiling down on you right now, make no mistake about it."

She'd been fighting tears all day, but her father's words had them flowing. "Daddy..." When he wiped a tear from his eyes, Renata hugged him tight. "I love you. I'm sorry, I know this isn't the way you imagined this."

He patted her back. "Nothing to be sorry for, Renata. You found your fella. He's a good man, a good fit—and I'm mighty fond of the way he loves you and his boy. Besides, I'm tickled pink to have more grandbabies coming. These will be extra special because they're yours." He smiled down at her. "I'd say today is just about perfect."

"Isn't it?" she agreed.

He hugged her again, pressing a kiss to her cheek. "Well, let's not keep your fella waiting. He's been pacing the floor, itching for you to get here."

She swallowed, remembering the love in his eyes last night. He hadn't been happy about saying goodnight, knowing he wouldn't see her until the wedding. But tradition mattered to her family and to her, so he'd relented. Because, he reminded her, if she was happy, he was happy.

"If I didn't see how Ash feels about you, I might have some reservations about all this. But that boy?" He smiled at her. "It's in his eyes. Plain as day. Does a father's heart good to see, let me tell you." He kissed her cheek. "Enough talking."

The doors opened and, beyond the small crowd of Boones, Ash's mother and Betty, Ash Carmichael stood, shifting from foot to foot, looking every bit the nervous groom. But when he saw her, she heard her father's voice. There was tenderness in his eyes—and so much more.

His sudden swallow. The tightening of his jaw. The rapid blinking. That this man wanted to be here, wanted to marry her, filled her with pride. And love. So much love.

His smile was all for her.

Someone, probably Eden, had created an impromptu aisle—with rose petals. Her father led the way, his hand covering hers. She heard the whispers and mur-

murings of her brothers, their wives and the passel of kids packing the small one-room building, but had no idea what they were saying. All she saw, all that mattered, was Ash.

Her father placed her hand in Ash's.

"How the hell did I get so lucky?" Ash's hands were shaking.

"Make sure you never forget it," her father said. "I'm giving you my daughter but I won't hesitate to take her back."

Ash nodded, grinning widely. "I give you my word that will never be necessary."

"We ready to get this wedding started?" Judge Mack McCoy asked. "I hear there's some sort of shindig over at Cutter's tonight and I don't want to be late."

Ash considered himself a patient man. But since his proposal, he'd been a man with a purpose. Now that she'd said yes, nothing was more important than marrying her. And now, with her hand in his, the fear that she'd back out, change her mind, began to fade away. Just like everything that had to do with Renata Boone, today had turned into something altogether unexpected. And wonderful.

She was wonderful.

Now she was there, wearing her boots and a smile that shook him to the bone. Holding her hand in his melted whatever lingering fears he had. He was here for her, because she was home. This place, this town, this family. He'd been given a second chance at a good life and he was going to grab on with both hands and hold tight.

She was what he wanted. Needed.

And this was perfect. Almost. "Wait," he said, turning toward his mother.

"Da," Curtis said, reaching for him, his starched button up pulling free from his pressed khaki pants.

"Yep, you gotta help me with something," he said, bracing his son against his hip and facing Renata. "We're a package deal."

There were tears in Renata's eyes. "I wouldn't have it any other way."

Curtis clapped his hands, bouncing in his arms.

"I know. We get to keep her." He laughed. "I'm happy, too."

Renata shook her head, but her smile was something else.

"Now we're ready?" Mack asked.

Ash took her hand in his and squeezed, earning him a smile. "We're ready."

Mack McCoy was a man of few words and Ash was thankful for it. When Mack asked for rings, Ash pulled the two gold bands he'd purchased for them from the pocket on Curtis's little black vest and held them out. What surprised them both was Curtis. He leaned forward, holding his arms out for Renata. And she took him, holding him close—like it was the most natural thing in the world. Their vows were short and sweet and, before he knew it, he and Renata were declared man and wife.

"Wait," he said again, handing Curtis back to his

mother, causing a round of laughter from those gathered. "Better," he said, sliding his arms around her. "Mrs. Carmichael."

She smiled up at him and wound her arms around his neck.

"Kid friendly, please," Archer called out, setting off a round of groans, slaps and laughter from her side of the family.

"Buzzkill," Ash said, pressing a gentle kiss against her mouth. He'd behave, for the moment. Now that they were married, he could kiss her wherever and whenever he damn well pleased.

"What's that smile about?" she asked.

"All the perks of being married to you." His hands cradled her face.

Her cheeks blossomed with color.

"I just need a few signatures," Mack interrupted. "Then we can get this show on the road."

It didn't take long to make everything legal. But helping load up the truckloads of kids and family members for the short drive to Cutter's did.

"Can we walk?" Renata asked, smoothing a hand over her stomach.

He nodded. "Whatever you want." Besides, leaving his truck where it was might make for an easier getaway.

The mothers unpacked the stroller, bundled Curtis up and led the way, stopping every now and then to look at a shop.

It was a pretty day. The sun was out. And he wanted to walk down Main Street with his new bride. "Happy?" he asked Renata.

She nodded.

His fingers threaded with hers, caressing the back of her hand with his thumb. "Can't keep your hands off me," he teased. He sure as hell couldn't keep his hands off her.

She flashed him a cheeky grin. "I can't?"

He chuckled. "You're up to no good."

"I am?" she asked. "How do you know what I'm thinking?"

He squeezed her hand. "Just lucky, I guess."

"Is that what you call it?" she asked, her brows arching. "I'd call it shameless."

The walk to Cutter's was interrupted every few feet. The shopkeepers and business owners of Stonewall Crossing wanted to offer congratulations—making their short walk longer. Not that he minded. He'd have been fine skipping the reception altogether. What he wanted, more than anything, was time with his new wife.

Renata had asked that they postpone their honeymoon until the new year, and since he didn't want to spend the holidays away from Curtis, he'd agreed. Besides, the holidays were a time for family. What better opportunity to start building memories and traditions as a new family?

"What's your favorite color?" she asked.

He chuckled. "What?"

She tugged on his arm. "What's your favorite color?" She looked up at him, expectant.

"Blue," he answered. Blue, like her eyes.

She nodded.

"Why?" he asked.

"I don't know. I realized I didn't know. It's something a woman should know about her husband." She shrugged, her eyes searching his. "There's still a lot we don't know about each other. It popped into my head, so I asked."

He nodded. "Keep asking."

She smiled. "Oh, I will."

"Your favorite color?"

Her brows rose high. "Brown. Most of my favorite things are brown. My saddle. My favorite hat." She pointed at her feet. "My boots."

He shook his head.

"What?" She tugged on his arm again.

"You're full of surprises." He wrapped his arm around her shoulder and steered her across the street to Cutter's.

"That's a bad thing?" she asked.

"No. It's a Renata thing." He stopped on Cutter's wide front porch and turned her to face him. "I wouldn't have it any other way."

"That's good because I think what Judge McCoy just did was some sort of legally binding agreement." She reached up to run her fingers through his hair.

"Whoa, now." Ryder Boone stood in the doorway. "These things here are called windows. And people can see through them." He pointed back and forth between them. "That right there will have to wait until later."

Ash stooped to whisper "Not too much later."

"I was thinking the same thing." Renata laughed, pressing one soft, sweet kiss to his lips.

Epilogue

"Come on, Ash." Renata stood, one hand on each of Fisher's boys.

"Timer is set," Ash said, running back to his spot beside her. "Watch for the flash. Everyone smile. It'll take about five."

The camera flashed and Renata let the boys go, laughing as they raced around the couch. "I wish I had that sort of energy."

"If you tried to do that, we'd wind up in the hospital." Ash eyed the boys and shook his head, placing his hand on her round stomach. "Let's give them as much time as they need."

"Agreed." Her father stood. "Can we cut the cake now?"

"Yes, Teddy, we can cut the cake." Clara touched his cheek. "What a romantic."

"I was going to feed you a bite." Her father laughed.

"Five years." Hunter shook his head. "Time sure does fly. Happy Anniversary, Dad." He hugged Clara.

Renata hugged her stepmother. "Seems like you've been a part of the family for longer."

"It does." Clara smiled.

Josie bounced her and Hunter's daughter, Ana, on her hip. "Here's to many more."

Hunter nodded, slipping his arm around his wife and kissing his daughter's head. "Many."

Kylee patted the back of her newborn. "Fisher tells me you two are taking an actual vacation?"

Fisher shrugged. "It's possible I dreamed that. I don't think Dad's ever taken a vacation—unless it had something to do with a rodeo or stock show."

"You didn't dream it." Clara laughed.

"I'm impressed, Clara. I think Fisher's right. Dad's never ventured very far. Glad to see him have an adventure." Renata's stomach tightened, but she ignored it. This was Clara and her father's day. She'd already had two false alarms—she didn't want to ruin the party with another one.

"Clara's taking him to meet her sisters," Eden said, keeping one eye on her girls. "In Austria."

"You own a passport?" Archer asked his father, taking the hand that Eden offered him.

"He does now." Clara laughed.

"I'm impressed, Dad." Ryder had his arms wrapped

around Annabeth. "I never thought you'd leave all your grandkids."

Her father frowned. "We won't be gone that long."

"He's teasing you." Renata shot her brother a look. "You two deserve time, just the two of you." Her stomach clamped down so hard she didn't have time to swallow down her groan.

All eyes turned her way.

"Renata?" Ash turned her to face him.

"It's just another false alarm," she assured him. "It has to be." But her stomach contracted again, harder this time.

"Load up," Fisher called out.

"No, don't load up," she argued. "Ash will call you if this is real. Stay, have cake." She winked at her father.

"She's right," Ash agreed. But she didn't miss the wink he gave Fisher.

"You two are terrible," she said, clinging to Ash's hand.

"Ash, you two head out. We'll be there soon." Her father patted her cheek. "You got this."

It took a good five minutes to make their goodbyes. Her water broke on the way to Ash's truck. "Curtis? I don't want him waking up and we're both gone."

"I'll call my mom and Betty when we get to the hospital." He kissed her hand as he backed the truck up. "They'll bring him up after his nap. You don't need to worry about a thing."

She nodded, squeezing his hand. He was acting calm, cool and collected, but she saw the concern in his eyes. "I love you."

"And I love you," he said, picking up speed as they neared the hospital.

Dr. Farriday said it was one of the fastest twin deliveries she'd ever seen. Eleven hours was quite enough for her—and Ash.

John Theodore and Sara Jean were born eight minutes apart.

And when they were wheeled into her room from the nursery, there was no shortage of arms ready and willing to pass the babies around. Her father was beaming with pride. Her brothers fought over who looked most like who. And Fisher told her it was only fair that JT was a big brother—since she'd always be his big sister.

Renata lay back against her pillows, staring around her crowded room. There was so much love here.

"You okay?" Ash asked, bending low to kiss her.

"A little overwhelmed," she admitted, smiling up at him. "We're blessed, Ash. To have all this."

"And each other." He kissed her again. "Every day is an adventure."

"Unexpected?" she asked.

"In the best possible way." He chuckled.

She stared up at him, marveling—as always—that this wonderful man was her husband. "I'm glad you chose to love me, Ash."

"I'm not sure I had a choice, Renata. You belong here," he whispered, pressing her hand over his heart. The love in his eyes shone bright. "And I belong to you."

* * * * *

SPECIAL EXCERPT FROM

H HARLEQUIN®

SPECIAL EDITION

*When Shania Stewart tells Deputy Daniel Tallchief that
he needs to lighten up with his wild younger sister,
the handsome lawman doesn't know whether to
ignore her or kiss her. But Shania knows.
It's going to take a carefully crafted lesson plan
to tutor this cowboy in love.*

Read on for a sneak preview of
The Lawman's Romance Lesson,
the next great book in USA TODAY *bestselling author
Marie Ferrarella's Forever, Texas miniseries.*

Shania flushed as she raised her eyes toward Daniel. "I don't usually babble like this."

Daniel found the pink hue that had suddenly risen to her cheeks rather sweet. The next second, he realized that he was staring. Daniel forced himself to look away. "I hadn't noticed."

"Yes, you had," Shania contradicted. "But I think that it's very nice of you to pretend that you hadn't." When she heard Daniel laugh softly to himself, she asked him, "What's so funny?" before she could think to stop herself.

"I'm not accustomed to hearing the word *nice* used to describe me," he admitted.

Didn't the man have any close friends? Someone to bolster him up when he was down on himself? "You're kidding."

The lopsided smile answered her before he did. "Something else I'm not known for."

She pretended that he was a student and she did a quick assessment of the man before her. "You know you're being very hard on yourself."

"Not hard," he contradicted. "Just honest."

She had no intention of letting this slide. If he had been one of her students, she would have done what she could to raise his spirits—or maybe it was his self-esteem that needed help.

"Well, I think you're nice—and you do have a sense of humor."

"If you say so," Daniel replied, not about to dispute the matter. He had a feeling that arguing with Shania would be pointless. "But just so you know, I'm not about to chuck my career and become a stand-up comedian."

She grinned at his words. "See, I told you that you had a sense of humor," she declared happily.

Don't miss
The Lawman's Romance Lesson *by Marie Ferrarella,*
available April 2019 wherever
Harlequin® Special Edition books and ebooks are sold.

www.Harlequin.com

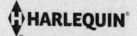

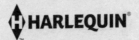

Love Harlequin romance?

DISCOVER.

Be the first to find out about promotions,
news and exclusive content!

 Facebook.com/HarlequinBooks

Twitter.com/HarlequinBooks

 Instagram.com/HarlequinBooks

Pinterest.com/HarlequinBooks

ReaderService.com

EXPLORE.

Sign up for the Harlequin e-newsletter and
download a free book from any series at
TryHarlequin.com.

CONNECT.

Join our Harlequin community to share
your thoughts and connect with other
romance readers!
Facebook.com/groups/HarlequinConnection

**ROMANCE WHEN
YOU NEED IT**

HSOCIAL2018

Rewar
love

Earn points on your purchase of new Harlequin
books from participating retailers.

Turn your points into **FREE BOOKS**
of your choice!

Join for FREE today at
www.HarlequinMyRewards.com.

Harlequin My Rewards is a free program (no fees)
without any commitments or obligations.

MYR18